STORK

Shane McKenzie

Cover Art by Jim Agpalza
Edited by Ashley Thomas

Printed in the USA

WARNING:
This book contains scenes and subject matter that are disgusting and disturbing; easily offended people are not the intended audience.

JOIN MY MAILING LIST NOW
FOR EXCLUSIVE OFFERS BY VISITING:
shanemckenziehorror.substack.com

FOR SIGNED BOOKS, MERCHANDISE,
AND EXCLUSIVE ITEMS VISIT:

www.McHorror.net

This book is for the parents out there. Isn't it crazy the shit we'll do for our kids?

And for my wife Melinda who, at the time of this publication, has fought by my side for eighteen years. She is the Batman of our dynamic duo, and I am just a little brown Robin in yellow short-shorts.

McHorror
STABBY
Meals

Suzey woke to a searing pain in her abdomen that needled down to her womanhood. Even through the sharp pains, the grogginess of unconsciousness still muddied her mind, and she writhed in the cool sheets of her bed. She moaned, moving her arms and legs as if she were making a blanket angel.

It wasn't until her brain registered the wet warmth surrounding her, coating her legs and soaking her nightgown heavy, that she sat up and gasped. Her arms immediately wrapped around the small bulge of her belly, cradling it. She rocked herself for a moment, the room still too dark to see what she feared was happening.

"No… no, no, no…" Tears flooded her eyes and rolled down her cheeks. Strings of saliva connected her upper and lower lips as she wept, longing for Eddie's embrace. She reached to his side of the bed anyway, ran her damp hands over the dip there.

"Nnnooo…"

The pain lanced through her body again, a violent pulsing that refused to let up. A high-pitched whine squeezed from her throat and she kicked her legs, her heels shoving the comforter away.

She crawled across the bed and twisted the knob on the lamp. Sickly yellow light spilled into the room and revealed to her what she already knew was there. Just the sight of the blood-soaked sheets and comforter birthed a scream from the depths of her stomach. She rolled out of the bed and landed hard on her side. Blood stained her hands—darkest at her fingertips.

The carpet wiped some of the blood away as she crawled toward the discarded jeans ly-ing in a heap by the bedside table. She fished for her phone, choking on her sobs and sniffling. It nearly slipped from her slick hand but she squeezed it tight—she had to dial Eddie's number three times due to her trembling finger.

It rang forever and she was sure he was asleep, that he wouldn't answer. "Hey, baby? Kinda late, isn't it?"

"E-Eddie... oh, God."

She dropped the phone as she wept harder than ever. Just the sound of Eddie's tinny voice made everything feel more real, and his panic crackled from the phone on the floor, his tone growing more frantic by the second. She swiped it back up and lightly pressed it to her ear.

"Jesus, Suzey! What's going on? Are you all right?!"

"Eddie... it's happened again... It h-happened ag-again... What's wrong with me?!"

There was such a long silence on the other end, she thought Eddie had hung up. In that quick instant, she imagined him leaving her, finding another woman—a better woman. Someone who could give him what he wanted, someone whose body wasn't a wasteland, a barren desert. And she wasn't even mad at him. She understood.

"Are you okay, baby?" The deep, sleep-thick voice startled her. "Are you hurt?"

She took a deep breath, wiping her face across her arm. "There's pain, just like before. B-b-blood everywhere."

He sniffed, exhaled. "I'm on my way. First flight I can get, I'm on it, okay?"

She nodded, her face contorting in preparation for more tears. "Okay."

"We're going to be okay, sweetie. We'll make it through this, do you understand?"

A cry pushed out of her, quiet but full of pressure. Then a hard gasp followed by rhythmic whimpers.

"Suzey, listen to me. I need you to be strong. We both need to be strong."

"I-I know…"

"I'll be there before you know it… we'll figure this out, okay? We'll… we'll…"

His voice trailed off and Suzey hung up before he had a chance to say another word. It was all her fault, she knew. She didn't need any doctor to tell her that.

It's always been my fault, she thought. *Always will be.*

The stork only brings the souls of children to worthy mothers.

Her grandmother's voice boiled in her brain, and she melted to the floor and cried face-down into the carpet.

I'M CURSED

Suzey paced in front of the door—she'd been doing so for hours. She still couldn't bring herself to change the sheets and had only just showered an hour ago.

The blood caked over her hands had dried into crimson gloves, and she'd had to scrub with her nails to get it off. They still looked too pink to her, the blood of her lifeless child tattooed there forever. A constant reminder that she was not destined for motherhood, not fertile enough to create life.

Eddie had gone out of town for business but was only a two-hour flight away. *Give him another two for transportation from the airport to the apartment*, she told herself.

Her eyes periodically darted toward the microwave clock and, according to her calculations, he should have been home at least an hour ago. Every time she heard a car door slam, her stomach dropped, but Eddie just wouldn't come across the threshold.

Another throbbing spear of pain shot through her body, and she hugged her stomach, widened her nostrils, and breathed deeply.

The door flew open. Eddie, sweat beading across his face like crystallized acne, fell to his knees when he locked eyes with Suzey. His bottom lip hopped up and down as he extended his arms and invited her to join him on the floor. And when she did, they wept into each other's shoulders.

"I'm—I'm so sorry… I'm so s-sorry…" Her throat burned from crying so long and hard. Eddie squealed as he sobbed, then seemed to catch himself, tightening his body and squeezing her.

"We're okay, baby. Yeah? Okay, okay. We're fine." His fingers combed her hair, and he peppered her forehead with kisses. He dropped his mouth to hers and they kissed, long and hard, lubricated and sloppy with tears.

"It's me. I know it's me. You shouldn't be with me, E-Eddie." She shook her head and pulled away from his embrace. "I'm cursed. My body… it's no good."

"I don't want to hear that. Don't even start with that bullshit, okay?" All sadness was absent from his voice now. "You're my wife. I love you, Suzey. I love you."

His eyes coasted to the mess in the bedroom. The austere expression on his face oozed into a grimace. He climbed to his feet and traipsed toward it with wide eyes, his steps stiff and tentative. He didn't cry, didn't make a sound.

Suzey followed him, her hand covering her mouth. She forced herself to remain calm as she awaited his reaction. Her hand crept upward toward his shoulder and balled up the fabric of his polo. Then she saw the pink hue staining her skin and she quickly removed the hand, rubbing her palms together until they hurt.

Eddie ran his fingertips over the thickening blood on the bed. "H-hospital… we need to get you to the hospital right away! C-come on, let's—"

"No, no hospital. It's not as b-bad as it looks. I'm fine, it's—"

"Fine? Baby, look at all this blood! No, we're going, we're going right now."

"Ed, no. We've been through this before. The doctors, they can't help. I'm fine, I just want to be here... with you. Okay?"

He sat down on the edge of the bed, ignoring the blood soaking into his pants. What might have been a smile eased over his mouth, but his eyes showed exhaustion.

He nodded and patted the bed, keeping his eyes glued to Suzey's.

She stepped closer, refusing to let the blood touch her as she leaned into him.

"We can try again. Okay? We'll just try again, that's all," Eddie said.

She crossed her arms over her stomach and shook her head. "No. No, we can't. *I* can't. What's the point?"

He reached for her, but she pulled away. "Don't talk that way. It's what we always—"

"This isn't what I wanted. Not like this." Her heavy head hung from her limp neck. "This is the third one—the *third*. It's just... not meant to be."

He stood and forced her to let him hold

her. "We need to change things—our surroundings. What do you say we leave this fucking place, hmm?"

She tried to shove away, but he tightened his hold on her. Her head leaned back and she locked eyes with him. "What do you mean?"

A smile—a real smile—lit his face. "That's right. I got it. I was going to tell you before… before all this. But, baby, I got it."

"Oh my god, Eddie." They hugged each other for what seemed like hours, but she didn't want to let him go. Not ever. "So what does this mean?"

A kiss, soft and loving. "Well, for one thing, it means we need to go house shopping."

WHERE BABIES COME FROM

The electrical cord whipped through the air and whacked Suzey on her bare left buttock.

Whap!

She clenched her teeth and squeezed the tears from her eyes with a hard squint. But she didn't cry out—it would only make Grandma hit harder.

Another one. *Whap!* This one on the lower back, stinging like a hundred bees.

Drool escaped her lip and pooled beneath her. She gasped through her nose and the wall of her teeth.

"Now why would you ask a question like that, hmm? What could have put that thought in your head? A young girl like you already a whore? Just like your mother?"

Whap!

"*Nghh*… a girl at school," Suzey squealed. "I-I didn't believe her. I didn't!"

Grandma stepped around Suzey's crouched body, the cord wrapped around her hands like brass knuckles. The veins on the back of her hands bulged from the pressure, looking ready to burst. "Pull your pants up."

Suzey wiped her face and did as she was told. She hugged her knees, trying not to look Grandma in the eye.

"Do I need to remind you? I haven't told you enough times?"

Suzey had been told the story about the stork many times. Grandma's way of explaining the uncomfortable subject of where babies come from, or at least that's what the girl at school, Amanda, had said.

"A stork? And you really believe that? What are you, stupid or something?"

"The stork brings the souls of babies to worthy mothers," Suzey said to Grandma. "That's what I told her."

But Amanda had only laughed. *"I know how babies are made. I've seen my parents doing it, lots of times. My dad, he puts his thing in there, and my mom, she screams because it hurts so bad."*

Confused and embarrassed, Suzey had come straight home after school and asked Grandma about it—big mistake.

"This girl," Grandma said, "has no soul. The stork would have never brought a child's precious soul to a mother like that."

"L-like me?"

Grandma scowled. "Yes, Suzey, just like you. Your mother was a whore, I told you. The stork wouldn't bring a child's soul to a whore."

Suzey chewed on her tongue and hugged her knees. "But…"

"But what?"

"If I don't have a soul… how am I alive?"

The old woman chuckled, pulling the wire taut. "You've got evil in you. The devil's spawn is what you are."

NOT EVERYTHING IS GREAT

"I love it!" Suzey clapped, turned, and wrapped her arms around Eddie's neck.

He snickered. "Yes, I think she likes it."

Suzey released her husband and faced the realtor who beamed and extended her hand. Eddie shook it, rattling the gold bracelets on her arm.

"Fantastic," the realtor said, then shook Suzey's hand. "Let me just draw up the paperwork, and we'll be in touch. You'll be in your new home before you know it."

"Can we stay? I mean, just a little longer?

Look around some more?" Suzey's eyes bounced from the woman to Eddie.

Eddie faced the realtor, raised his eyebrows, and shrugged.

"Yes, of course. Feel free." The rotund realtor waddled off and out the front door.

Eddie grabbed Suzey by the shoulders and squeezed. "You really like it?"

"Oh my God, it's incredible!" She ran into the kitchen, hopped up and sat on the granite-top island. "Just look at this kitchen. I never imagined I could ever live in a place like this."

He joined her, running his fingertips over the countertops, the same dark granite as the island. "I know, me either. But get used to it, baby. There's nothing but great things in our future."

Not everything is great.

But she forced those thoughts back down. No negativity right now, no pessimism. The doctor's visit, after the latest miscarriage, had been cookie cutter. The same old shit, just like she knew it would be, but with a hint of accusation.

If it happens again, she told herself, *no fucking doctors. They can't do a damn thing for me.*

She kicked off the island and landed hard in Eddie's arms. Her lips, slickened by her tongue, pressed against his, and they kissed long and deep. His hands crept down to her ass and squeezed—his tongue inched into her mouth and found hers.

She pulled away, putting her hand to her chest. "My goodness."

He looked around as if they were criminals conspiring. "I have an idea."

Her hand found the bulge in his pants and massaged it. "So do I."

In the next moment, she was back on the island, the granite cold against her naked skin. Eddie was on her, inside of her, and she didn't care who heard her screams.

SOONER OR LATER

The movers lugged her dresser through the front hallway and angled it into the bedroom. She smiled and nodded at them as they went back out for the next load.

"I feel bad making them do everything," Suzey said as she unpacked the box labeled KITCHEN STUFF. "Maybe we should help out."

Eddie wrapped an arm around her. "Shit, for what I'm paying them, they should cook us dinner too."

She laughed. "Look at us. Couple of big shots, don't even have to move our own stuff."

"That's right, baby."

Eddie directed a large Hispanic man upstairs with the boxes labeled BOOKS. "And I finally have my own office." He cut the tape wrapped around a shoebox, pulled the pistol out, and struck a pose. "Hey, Suze. Do I look like James Bond when I do this?"

She gasped. "Put that thing away, idiot. You're gonna freak the movers out." A frown contorted her expression. "Thought we decided to get rid of it."

"Not until I know we're safe enough without it."

"Ed, we're in the suburbs here. I don't think the joggers and dog walkers pose much of a threat to our safety."

"Never know, that's all I'm saying." He tucked the gun back into the box and set it aside.

Suzey sighed and shook her head, then decided to just let it go. She stacked plates and placed them in one of the cupboards, then changed her mind and used the one across the kitchen. "I can't wait to use that track out there. Looks pretty nice."

"Mm-hmm, and the pond is pretty too," he said. "Think I saw one duck floating around in there. You think he drowned all the other ducks? A serial killer duck, that's what we got."

She snorted and slapped him on the arm. "You're retarded."

He clicked his tongue and smiled, then wrapped his arm around her lower back, pulling her in for a kiss. "How do you feel?"

"What do you mean?"

"You know." He pressed his palm against her stomach. "You... okay?"

She jerked away and started pulling glasses out of another box, her eyebrows curled. "Can we not talk about that right now? Can't I just enjoy our new home? Shit."

A long silence fell over them, sprinkled with clinking glasses and the shuffling of the movers' feet as they came and went.

He's going to find out sooner or later, and then you'll lose everything. You'll be alone, just like you deserve.

"You're right. I'm sorry." He hugged her from behind, leaning his face on the back of her head.

She spun and kissed him. "Don't worry about it. Now quit fucking around and help a sister out."

They smiled at each other, kissed again, and then went back to unloading boxes.

A LITTLE DEAD BABY

"I know the pond in which all the little children lie, waiting till the storks come to take them to their parents," Grandma said, and then turned the page.

Suzey sat cross-legged on the floor, listening to the story she had heard so many times before: *The Storks* by Hans Christian Andersen. Out of all the tales Grandma told her, this one scared her the most.

"There lies in the pond a little dead baby who has dreamed itself to death, said the mother. We will take it to the naughty boy, and he will cry because we have brought him a little dead brother." Grandma's eyes slid from the page to Suzey's face. "You see? Bad people don't get healthy babies. They get dead babies, or in your case, an empty, soulless shell."

Suzey's backside still hurt from the night before, but she knew what happened after story time. A tear dripped from her eye in anticipation for the lashings. She felt her chest and stomach, flexing her fingers.

"But I don't feel evil. I just feel… normal."

Grandma slammed the book shut and laid it on top of the pile of children's books beside her. Every one of them about storks and babies. "Evil would feel normal to you. You wouldn't know what *real* normal felt like." She stood and retrieved her cord from the end table. "Now drop your pants and lift your shirt, child."

DAUGHTER OF A WHORE

Eddie grabbed fistfuls of hair from either side of his head as Suzey bucked on top of him, slamming her groin into his with violent rhythm. Her eyes were all white, pupils rolled to the back of her head, and with each bed-shaking thrust, she bared her teeth and growled.

The growling was new, but Eddie wasn't going to complain.

When Eddie tried to flip her over to her hands and knees so he could take her from behind——be the dominant one for a while——she would go rigid, squeeze her vaginal walls like a tightening fist around his cock.

Her small hands shoved him in the middle of the chest, clawing and pulling at his chest hairs. A low rattle crackled from her throat as she tossed her head back, tongue circling her lips, hands reaching for the ceiling.

Eddie just lay back, gripped his wife by the flesh of her hips, and enjoyed the ride.

***

The sound of the shower brought Suzey gasping into consciousness, the hiss and splatter of water mingling with Eddie's whistling. The sheets were a haphazard mess on the bed, and as she collected herself, Suzey realized she was naked.

Again?

She scooted backward, wincing at the dull ache between her legs. She reached down and touched herself—Eddie's seed coated her.

You're the daughter of a whore.

It had happened countless times before, her mind swirling away to another world while her body did unspeakable things. When she'd gotten serious with Eddie, leaving her former life behind, she'd hoped it would stop. But here she was, filled with her husband's ejaculate, with no memory of what they'd done. She could only hope she had pleased him, and by the tune of his whistle, she supposed she had.

She couldn't help but feel violated in some way, though she knew it wasn't Eddie's fault.

Do I just lay there like some wide-eyed corpse while he ravages my body? she wondered. *Or does some other part of me take over... some other consciousness?*

You are the devil's spawn.

And how many times have we had sex without my knowledge? she thought. *Could there be incidents that I don't know of?*

The thought chilled her, embarrassed her. Sure, there were times she could remember, times when she'd initiated it, but more often than not, she was tossed back into her body after the deed had been done.

The water cut off and the curtain swooshed open.

Suzey couldn't face him. She was filled with a thick shame she couldn't shake off, so she rolled over, her back facing the restroom, and pretended to sleep.

PLUS SIGN

"Well?" Eddie's voice was muffled from the other side of the bathroom door.

Suzey had been pacing, then finally plucked the test from the top of the toilet tank. She didn't know what she wanted to see. The plus sign had filled her and Eddie with joy so many times before only to disappoint. That plus sign began to signify something else to her, an ominous harbinger of future heartbreak.

"Jesus Christ, Suze, please say something."

"It's... uh." She almost said negative. The tip of her tongue was at the roof of her mouth behind her teeth, but she stopped herself. "It's positive."

"What?"

"Positive, it's fucking positive, okay?" She tossed the plastic stick to the trash, sat down on the toilet seat, and faced the blank wall. Her stomach was staticky, and she felt like she might start hyperventilating. The points of her elbows dug into the meat of her thighs as she leaned over.

"This is great, baby!"

Silence. The doorknob rattled.

"Suze? What's the matter?"

I have no soul. I'm the daughter of a whore who followed in her mother's footsteps. I'm not a fit mother, and the stork won't stop bringing me dead babies.

"Suzey... you're freaking me out. Let me in."

She took one final deep breath, rose from the toilet, and opened the door. Before Eddie could squeeze into the restroom with her, she sidestepped past him. She went straight for their bedroom where she flopped down on the bed and hid her sorrowful face in the feather pillow.

The bedsprings squeaked and a hand

found the back of her neck, massaging it. "You have nothing to worry about. It's going to be different this time, I just know it. I can feel it."

"Really? You can feel it, huh?" Suzey shook her head. "Bullshit."

His hand pulled away from her and the bed squeaked again. "You have to think positively, and I know how stupid that sounds to you. But seriously, I mean it."

"So what, I think happy thoughts and this baby won't die inside of me, is that it?"

"Either that or we both live in fear. What's the fucking point of that?"

She sat up and wiped her face. "I already live in fear, Ed. All the time. I…"

She almost told him everything, almost let it come spilling out like hot vomit. The moment she'd met Eddie, the nicest man she'd ever come across, she made the decision right then and there to keep her past a secret. It was something he didn't need to know, something that would only drive him away from her.

But she never expected him to propose to her, didn't even expect to agree to it. She definitely didn't expect them to try and have kids.

She was only a child when she'd decided never to have children. To stop the curse that her mother had started. Whores having whore children, all empty and soulless.

As she stared into Eddie's eyes and he stared back, waiting for her to continue, his hands fumbling with each other as he prepared for her next words, she just couldn't do it. She couldn't tell him. As far as he knew, she had no past. He had only asked about her family once, and Suzey had snapped at him, told him to mind his business—he never brought it up again.

"You're right. You're always right," she said and smiled at him. She held out her arms for him to join her, and he took the invitation and squeezed her tight. The smell of his musk tingled her loins, and she found herself kissing his neck, extending her tongue and bathing the creases.

"What are you doing?"

"What do you think I'm doing?" Her hand went to his zipper and pulled.

He jumped back up. "Are you serious right now?"

"What's your problem?"

He shook his head. "What's *my* problem?

Jesus Christ, Suzey." His footsteps were heavy as he stomped toward the bedroom door. "Why don't you get a hold of yourself, huh? I—I need to go… somewhere. I'll be back later."

She shook her head, mouth agape, and tried to find the words to make him stay, to make him explain himself. But nothing came to her, and she could only watch as her husband flung the door open and slammed it behind him, followed by his headlights swooshing into the home through the front windows as he backed out of the driveway and finally disappeared.

Her hands shook, her brain ached.

What the fuck is wrong with me?

You have no soul, Suzey. You're the devil's spawn.

WORTHLESS TRASH

Suzey finished her canned soup—the same flavor for the past month: tomato. She hated it but was given nothing else.

Her bare feet tickled on the carpet as she slid down the hall toward the living room where Grandma sat watching the news. The old woman rocked in her chair, sipping coffee with tight lips.

"G-Grandma?"

The rocking halted and the old woman's head spun slowly, her eyes hard and animated with the reflections of the television. "What are you doing out of your room?"

"I'm not tired. The sun's still out... why

do I have to stay in there?"

"Don't you talk to me in that tone, you little shit. Get back in there, right now."

Suzey nearly crumbled, as always, and did what she was told, but she bit her lower lip and crossed her arms. "No. I don't want to."

With a quick flick of her wrist, Grandma splashed the contents of her coffee cup into Suzey's face.

The scalding liquid covered her in agony and she screamed, fell to her knees, and wiped at her face, crying and kicking her legs. It felt like she was melting, like the skin was sizzling and dripping away.

Her breaths rattled out in tiny whisps. She blinked rapidly, her eyelids like open wounds.

"You don't talk back to me, you little bitch. The one that feeds you, takes care of you?! Even though you're worthless trash like your mother was!"

Suzey blinked up at the woman who trudged toward her, kicking the coffee cup out of the way to smash against the wall. Grandma's hand exploded out and slapped the side of Suzey's wounded face, then again on the other side.

Suzey's shriek felt like it would tear her

throat open. She cried in loud bursts of pain, bent over so her face was covered. "Why do you h-hate me?"

"I don't want you here. But the state says I don't have a choice about it, so here you are." A sharp kick to Suzey's side. "Didn't want your slut mother either. Girl was given the world and decided to follow the devil anyway. Then she spat *you* out, and *I* was given the burden of fucking raising you!"

Suzey could only cover her face and stomach as the flurry of blows rained down on her. She wished she wasn't evil, wished her mother wasn't a whore. Wished the stork would have brought her a soul.

I DESERVE WORSE

Eddie stumbled back into the home a few hours later. Suzey still sat on the bed—she hadn't moved since he'd stormed out.

She still couldn't figure out why he'd gotten so upset, but she knew she must have done something. Sweet Eddie, perfect Eddie, would never act out in that way unless it was deserved.

He nearly tripped into the bedroom but caught himself on the dresser before facing Suzey. The scent of liquor wafted into the room, an indulgence her husband rarely took part in, so she knew she had fucked up bad somehow.

"Hey," he said, then pulled his shirt off, kicked off his shoes, and sat on the bed beside her. "Baby, I-I'm sorry. I didn't m-mean—"

She scooted closer to him. "No, I'm sorry. It was… inappropriate. We had *just* found out we're pregnant. I don't know what I was thinking."

He shook his head and ran a hand through his hair. "No, it's not even that. It's just… I don't know, you've been—you've been different lately. I mean, in bed."

Oh God, what did I do?

"In bed?" She grabbed the comforter, pulled it over herself, and stared blankly at the wall.

"Don't get me wrong. I love it. I really do, but… You don't seem like yourself lately." He chuckled. "Shit, we'd already had sex three times today. And after the test came up positive… I don't know…"

Three times?

Suzey had no recollection of any of that. The last time she remembered actually having sex with him was on the kitchen island before they'd moved in. Now that she thought about it, the day had felt short, but she just figured they were busy unpacking, that time had gotten away from her. But three times?

God, she thought, *I have to tell him. He has to know.*

"Eddie? I—" On the tip of her tongue, nothing's been said yet, still time to turn back, change her mind.

No… no, it's time he knew. He deserves honesty.

After dating for two years and being married for one, she wondered if the information would ruin him, shatter any form of trust he ever had with her. But it was eating her alive, and if she didn't tell him soon, she felt the weight of it would crush her.

"What is it?"

"I—I have to tell you something. About my past. Something I was too scared to tell you before, really too scared to tell you now, but I think it's time you knew."

His eyes darkened and he shifted his weight, but she noticed he didn't get close to her, didn't smile or hold her like he usually did.

"When I was a little girl, before I can even remember… my mother was killed."

"Oh, Suze, I—"

"By her pimp. He shot her in front of me, from what my grandma said, but I don't remember that. I had to live with her, my grandma, and she hated me. Told me I didn't have a soul because I was the daughter of a whore… Said the stork doesn't bring souls to a whore's offspring."

"Oh, God. Baby—"

She held up a hand. "Please, Eddie. There's more… a lot more. I don't know how else to say this, so I'll just say it. She beat me, every day, told me the same stories, every day, always about the stork. I couldn't take it any more after a while, so I ran away. Lived on my own since I was twelve. Ran with a crowd I shouldn't have, but at the time, they seemed nice, took care of me." She paused, exhaled, massaged her forehead. "Eddie, I was a prostitute from the age of thirteen until I was about twenty."

Saying the words out loud was like spitting out rotten food. The words hung in the air like a cloud of gnats, and she watched them hit Eddie.

The man visibly flinched at the word *prostitute*, then seemed to sink into himself. He wouldn't look at her. She waited for him to respond, but he had become inanimate, so to avoid further awkwardness, she continued.

"My grandma always said I would follow in my mother's footsteps, and she was right. I believed her about everything for so long, still do to some degree. That I'm an evil person, that I have no soul. That's why whoring was so easy, I told myself. Because I'm not a normal person."

She paused again, waiting for him to interject, tell her she was wrong, that she was normal, that she wasn't evil. But nothing, not even the twitch of a finger.

"I got into drugs *bad*. I got pregnant… a few times. But I took care of them—aborted them." Her head felt like it was filling with hot air. Sweat coated her face and mixed with the tears. "Ten. I had ten abortions during that time."

His head turned. Eyes bore into her face. Jaw muscles twitched.

He's leaving me for sure now. I'm going to be all alone again and I deserve no better. I deserve worse.

"I had it in my head that it didn't matter. That my babies would be evil anyway. So I always aborted them. I—I…"

"Suzey…" His voice crackled in the air like

lightning.

She met his eyes and prepared for the shitstorm he was about to give her. Her tongue bled as her teeth mashed it down.

"Suzey… it's not your fault." And he crawled to her side of the bed and held her. The familiar feeling of his embrace was something she never thought she'd feel again, and his strong arms wrapped around her, his warmth smothering her. Even the hint of alcohol on his breath was welcome.

"You… you're not leaving me? You're not gonna divorce me?" She spoke into the crook of his arm and she wasn't sure if he'd heard her.

"Leave you? Suzey, I married you because I love you. You, the woman you are today, the woman I met three years ago." He pulled her away so he could look into her face. "Whatever you did, whatever happened in your past, I wouldn't change it. I wouldn't change it because it made you into who you are now, and that's who I love. That's who I'll *always* love."

She clutched him hard, palming the back of his head.

"Your grandma is to blame for all this shit.

Don't take this the wrong way, but I hope she's dead, hope she died terribly. Putting it in a child's head that she's evil? My god, Suze, I'm so sorry."

"You know, I have no idea if she's alive or not. I guess I don't want to know. If she is, she's probably in the same old house in Travis." The notion that the old woman could still be alive poked at something inside of her, filled her with a sense of dread, the same feeling she used to have just before the lashings started. And she couldn't tell Eddie that she still believed it to a degree, that she had no soul. That the stork would never stop bringing them dead children because she was a bad mother, a mother that had killed ten of her own babies.

"Well, for that bitch's sake, she better be dead. Because if I ever find her…"

Suzey chuckled lightly and hugged him again. "I love you so much, Ed. I was so scared to tell you. I thought you'd run out that door and never come back."

"We're family. I don't turn my back to my family." He pressed his hand to her belly, kissed her, and rested his forehead against hers. "How did you ever survive out there at such a young age?"

Her brow bunched up and she pursed her lips. "I just sort of became… numb. Blocked a lot of bad shit out, don't even remember most of it." She cupped his face in her hands. "And now I have you. I don't deserve you, did nothing in my life to warrant any form of happiness, but here you are, and here we are." She swept the room with her eyes, then glanced at her stomach. "And I'll never take any of it for granted."

After another round of hugs and kisses, they both lay on their backs, staring at the ceiling fan, fingers intertwined tightly between them.

"So I guess that explains it."

"Explains what?" she said.

He giggled, sniffed, and turned to his side so he could look at her. "Well… your sex drive. It's always been good, but lately, I don't know, it's been… potent."

"Potent?" She flushed with embarrassment. Even after all she'd already told him, and even though he took it better than she could have ever dreamed, she decided to leave out the part about the blackouts. If she told him she didn't even remember having sex with him most of the time, probably ninety percent of the time, he could take it the wrong way. The rest of it was in her past, but this problem was happening *now*.

"I don't know. You're like an animal." He scratched his head and looked away. "You've even been growling lately. It was kind of strange at first, I admit, but I'm starting to like it."

Growling?

She tightened her grip on his hand, unable to find the words to respond. So she just rolled over, laid her head on his chest, and within a few minutes, drifted off to sleep.

DOWNY FEATHERS

She woke in a dark room. Cold. Alone. She tried to sit up, but something was strapped over her chest, over her arms and legs, and she couldn't move an inch.

Not her bedroom—she wasn't in her home with her loving husband. The table she was lying on top of was hard, cold metal.

The lights above her cut on, like stadium lights, blinding her. Someone stood at the end of the metal table, someone she couldn't make out because of the harsh luminescence burning her eyeballs.

"Who are you? Where the fuck am I?"

The man tilted his head, studied her for a

moment, then stepped closer. Close enough for her to make out his face. Close enough for her to see the long, metal rod in his hand. The soft-looking, white feathers coating his arm.

"What… what are you doing? Let me out of here!"

The man walked to her side, sort of strutted, his neck bobbing back and forth as he stepped closer to her. He wore doctor's scrubs—white speckled with red. The downy feathers on his arms had the same crimson stippling. He wore a surgical mask over his face, but his eyes bore into her, huge and black and wet.

"Let me go… please let me go."

His head tilted again as he studied her, then he strutted back to the end of the table, back at her feet. He gripped something there, something Suzey couldn't see, but she could tell by the grinding sound and the motion of his body that it was some kind of crank.

And ever so slightly, her feet separated from each other, spread wider and wider.

A translucent film flicked over the massive orbs of the doctor's eyes, and her legs were spread wide until it felt like they would tear free at her hips like baked chicken drum-sticks.

The doctor showed her the metal rod again, the end thick with gore that wrapped around the tip and hung down in tattered ribbons.

And with a violent surge, he thrust it deep inside of her.

He swirled it around, pulled it out, and jammed it in again.

A TRUE STORY

"On the last house in a little village, the storks had built a nest, and the mother stork sat in it with her four young ones who stretched out their necks and pointed their black beaks—"

"Please, Grandma. Can't you tell me a different story?" Suzey said the words, though she knew she would probably regret it. She had begun to grow jaded by the constant punishments, fearing them less and less each day.

The old woman lightly shut the book and set it in her lap. She leaned forward and glared at her granddaughter. "Another story?"

"Please?"

Grandma set the book aside, shifted in her seat, and cleared her throat. "This is a true story."

Suzey sat cross-legged and rested her elbows on her knees.

"There once was a girl, a beautiful girl, with hair as yellow as banana peels…"

Suzey giggled at this image, then mashed her lips over her teeth when Grandma's eyes thinned to slits.

"This little girl was born into a good home, a happy home, and she had everything a little girl could ever want. But as she grew older, she became tempted by the devil, as we all are, but she succumbed to the evil, left her loving family behind to pursue the life of a harlot, to feed the mouths of those that hungered for flesh."

Suzey shook her head. "Okay, okay… read The Storks again, Grandma. I don't like this—"

"And then the harlot became pregnant from the seed of one of the hundreds of fornicators she'd bedded with. The stork had never visited her, never flew to her window, yet her belly continued to swell."

"Please… please stop now."

"And the whore's child came screaming into the world—empty, soulless… and evil. An abomination against God, against the great white stork. And then the harlot was killed, an inevitable end to a life of darkness."

"No more! Please shut up!"

"And then the child, the offspring of the devil, was thrust into the arms of her poor grandmother, the loving mother of the little girl who'd become a whore. But the grandmother knew it was a sign, a sign from God, from the stork. The abomination must be punished, and it is and always will be the grandmother's burden to show the whore's child the wrath of God."

Grandma's shoe caught Suzey's chin in a quick kick that sent the girl flying backward. Her teeth clicked and bit into her tongue, and she writhed on her back as blood spurted into her mouth.

Grandma rose from her chair, the hardback book in hand, and stood over Suzey. Her eyes showed how much hatred and resentment she held inside, and Suzey knew it would never stop, knew she had to get out of there before it got worse—before she was killed.

"We will revenge ourselves, whispered the young storks to each other," Grandma said, reciting the text from memory. And then the book was over her head.

It made a loud slapping sound when it struck Suzey's flesh, over and over and over again. Pink welts rose from her skin, and she tried to scurry away, but Grandma followed, hitting and kicking and grunting.

I'm an abomination. I deserve this. I deserve all of this.

SOME KIND OF OMEN

Suzey pulled the laces of her running shoes tight and headed out the door. The sun shone brutal heat down on top of her, but she soaked it in, relished in it.

It was a new day. She hadn't felt this good, this free, since the day she ran away from Grandma's, and even that couldn't compare to how she felt now.

Yes, when she'd married Eddie, when she turned her name from Bastion to Buddinger, it was an amazing feeling, a love that bubbled deep within her chest.

But now she truly felt free. The weight of her secret, her dark past, had been lifted. And she was still married. The man was so under-standing, it almost seemed unreal.

Now he knows. He knows and he accepts it. He accepts me *for who I really am.*

The devil's spawn.

She glanced at her belly, but it was too early to be showing. In her mind, she spoke to her unborn child, begged it to be healthy, to make it through. With her putrid secret out of her system, out in the air, the longing to be a mother—a *real* mother—had intensified.

She wanted nothing more than to cradle her baby in her arms and cover it with soft kisses. She imagined hugging Eddie as the two of them admired their son or daughter sleeping in their crib.

We're waiting for you, baby. Mommy and Daddy can't wait to meet you.

She pulled out her phone and dialed Eddie's number. By now, his plane would have landed, and though she didn't want to bother him, just thinking about him and their child filled her with so much excitement that she just had to hear his voice.

"Everything okay, baby?" Eddie said through the phone.

"I love you."

A chuckle. "I love you too, sweetie. That why you called?"

"You've been gone too long already. I miss you so bad." Suzey noticed his voice getting muffled for a moment as if he'd covered his phone with his hand.

"Sorry, Suze, I have to go. We've just arrived and we're already late for the meeting." More muffled talking, a raised voice. "I'll call you back as soon as I can, all right?"

"Okay, sorry. I love you."

There was no answer, and Suzey kept the phone to her ear for a bit before she realized he had hung up already.

A slight pang of jealousy flared within her, but she laughed it off.

He's at a business meeting, stupid. He just got off his plane and doesn't have time to baby-talk with his needy wife right now.

She slipped the phone back into her pocket and tucked the earbuds into her ears. Beethoven oozed into her head as she stretched in the driveway, bending herself in half and touching her toes.

The gravel track looped around a small pond with twin fountains shooting geysers of water into the air. A children's playground sat to the right of it, along with a basketball half-court and a swimming pool.

You see that, baby? We'll play there, together, as much as you want.

As she jogged around the first curve, she passed an elderly couple walking a pair of black labs. The dogs tugged against their leashes, desperate to reach Suzey and slap their tongues across her sweaty flesh. She smiled and gave the couple a slight wave before zooming past them toward the other side of the track.

The lone duck floated along, its orange feet kicking it across the surface. She wondered briefly why a duck would come here to be alone in such a small pond.

When she spotted the pond's other inhabitant, she nearly stumbled to the ground. Her heart jumped into her throat as she stared at the tall white bird standing on one foot at the edge of the water. Its long beak stood atop a stretched neck, and as Suzey approached, its head swiveled around to look at her.

What... what does this mean? How can this be?

The stork opened and flapped its wings, creating ripples across the surface of the pond as if displaying its power to her.

She almost pulled her phone out to call Eddie again but stopped herself as she took deep breaths on her way to a green plastic bench where she sat down. The bird walked along, its legs disappearing in the water as it poked its head through the surface, searching for a meaty meal.

"They're good luck, you know."

Suzey had been so entranced by the great bird that she didn't notice the woman standing just to her right who tossed torn bits of hot dog bun into the water. The woman's voice startled her, and Suzey flinched, then snickered at herself.

"I didn't mean to frighten you, missy," the old woman said with a smile. "Just making conversation is all."

Suzey stood and approached the woman. As she grew nearer, the woman's face molded into her grandmother's, all scowl and hate. But Suzey blinked it away until the woman's kind face unblurred and smiled at her again.

"No problem. I was just so… taken by the bird. B-beautiful." Her eyes pulled her head back toward the stork, but she caught herself and faced the woman again. "I'm Suzey…

just moved in a couple weeks ago."

The woman tossed the rest of her bread into the water, wiped her palms on her pants, and then approached Suzey with an outstretched hand. "You can just call me Mrs. Hopps. Welcome to the neighborhood, missy. Welcome."

Suzey turned again and watched the stork, which was standing back on its one leg, as still as a statue. "What's a stork doing at a place like this?"

"Oh, they just like the water," Mrs. Hopps said. "Not too uncommon around these parts for one to make its way to a pond like this one here. Gorgeous animal."

"Y-yeah," Suzey mumbled. "You said something about them being good luck?"

"Oh, yes. The white stork is a symbol of good luck and fertility. I'm sure you've heard that the stork brings babies to parents' homes, yes?"

Suzey hugged herself, eyes still on the bird. "Yeah, I might've heard something about that."

"They say babies' souls float in the water, and the storks scoop them up and deliver them." The woman laughed. "Greeks thought the stork was a baby thief, can you believe that? Took babies *away* instead of bringing them."

The stork suddenly burst into the air, raining droplets of water down into the pond, and took to the sky. Its wingspan stretched impressively wide as it flapped away. Suzey and the old woman stood in silence and watched for a couple of minutes, squinting against the sun.

"Looks like it's got a baby to deliver, yes?" Mrs. Hopps chuckled.

The duck quacked and picked the bits of floating, soggy bread from the surface, free to eat now that its larger pondmate was gone.

"Well," Mrs. Hopps said, "I think it's time for a turkey sandwich and a nice cold glass of iced tea." She pointed to the house just behind her. "That's me there. You up for it, missy?"

"Thank you, but I'll have to pass. Still got two miles to run if I'm gonna meet my goal."

"To be young again, I'll tell you. The trek from my door just to the pond here is enough for me. Knees can't take much more than that." The old woman beamed at Suzey and gave her a light pat on the shoulder. "Hope to see you around again, missy. Don't go hurting yourself, yes?"

"Okay, great to meet you, Mrs. Hopps. Maybe I can bring some hamburger buns next time, mix it up a bit."

A hearty chuckle. "Oh, yes. That sounds fine." And she waddled toward her home.

The people in the neighborhood, though mostly older folks, seemed extremely friendly. The thought of raising a family there filled Suzey with joy and made her excited for their future.

But she couldn't help but think the stork was some kind of omen. Out of all the places they could have lived, all the ponds that bird could have chosen, they met here, at this place.

The stork has never come to visit me before, never brought me a living baby.

Mrs. Hopps' words echoed within her skull, about how the Greeks considered the stork to be a baby thief. She looked to the sky, one hand acting as a visor, the other cradling her stomach.

You can't have my baby, you bastard. I'll kill you first.

DON'T FUCK THIS UP

"Where's your head at, Ed?"

"Huh? What's that?" Eddie's vision focused and he saw that all the ice in his drink had melted, watering down his Crown Royal.

"We just scored big on this account, and here you sit, looking like your dog got ran over." Buford slapped Eddie on the back and knocked his own drink back, spilling crooked lines of liquor down the sides of his neck.

Eddie sipped his drink, but the sting of it didn't sit right. "I don't know, man, I'm just... somewhere else right now."

Buford whispered something into the ear of the blonde bar rat in his lap, then slapped her ass as she waddled away.

He faced Eddie and chuckled. "These bitches see a man in a nice suit, and they get stars in their eyes, I tell you." He motioned toward the bartender for another drink. "Broad wanted a hundred bucks for a fuck. Anybody selling their pussy for that cheap probably has a dick, know what I'm saying?" Another slap to Eddie's back.

Eddie squeezed his eyes shut, pinching the bridge of his nose.

"I see the married life is setting in nicely, huh?" Buford said.

"You can say that."

"Believe me, I know, buddy. Tied the knot three times already, and this latest one... goddamn. Just the sound of her voice lately makes the hairs on the back of my neck stand up. You and Suzey, you been married, what, a year now?"

"Yep. Just celebrated our first anniversary a couple months ago. She's pregnant again, too."

"Again?" Buford eyed a redhead as she strutted by, his eyes pinned to her swaying ass with no attempt to disguise his gawking. "And you're nervous about being a father, is that it?"

"No, no, not at all. Actually, I've always wanted to be a father. But this isn't our first try. The babies just don't seem to survive more than a couple of months." Eddie shook his head and attempted another sip of his drink. "I'm… shit, I'm fucking terrified if I'm telling the truth. I don't know how much more of this either one of us can take."

"Shit, man. I'm damn sorry to hear that. And Suzey, she taking it okay?"

Eddie stared into his drink, swirling it around a few times. He didn't know how to answer that question. "She's handling it okay, I guess. It's just— she told me…"

"Yeah?"

Eddie bit his tongue, stood from the bar, and then tossed a ten on the counter. "Sorry, Buford, but I'm going to have to call it an early night. Head's just all over the place right now."

Buford's mouth hung open in disappointment. "You gonna leave me here to fend for myself with no wingman?"

"Maybe you should call your wife instead. Get some sleep."

Buford eyed another scantily clad female as he bit his bottom lip. "You handle your marriage woes your way, I'll handle 'em mine." He raised his drink. "Have a good night, fucker. And try to celebrate a bit, huh?

Order some fucking room service or something. We did good today, buddy. And it's time to get paid."

Eddie just shook his head and waved, then weaved his way through the bar crowd and out into the warm night. As he crossed the street toward his hotel, he pulled out his phone and saw that Suzey had called three times.

I'll just tell her the meeting went late, that I couldn't get away.

He couldn't bring himself to call her back. The sound of her voice was something he craved, but right now, he needed time to think. Drinks at the bar had seemed like the perfect way to calm down, to relax a bit and get his mind off things. But it had the opposite effect.

The chaotic sounds of the bar, along with Buford's constant chattering, were all just static in the back of Eddie's mind—Suzey's words banged inside of his skull like freshly fired bullets.

Initially, what he'd said to her was true. He loved her, and no matter what had happened in her past, no matter what mistakes she'd made, it wouldn't change the way he felt about her.

The love he held for his wife was like nothing he'd ever experienced. Sure, he'd had girlfriends, even a couple of serious relationships he'd thought might stretch on into marriage and eventually children. But when he'd met Suzey, it felt like a dream.

How could a girl be this perfect? he had asked himself. *And why in God's name would she be interested in me?*

Because she's an ex-hooker, that's why.

Eddie clenched his teeth as he entered the hotel lobby. The ride in the elevator was awkward as a young couple dry-humped in the corner, but he kept his eyes on the plastic number discs as they lit up one by one. When he finally reached his floor and the doors cracked open, he nearly dove out.

He remembered how he and Suzey used to be the same way. Just couldn't wait to jump each other's bones. They would be half-naked by the time they got to his or her place, shedding the rest of their clothing as they shoved through the door.

Always such a strong sex drive, my Suzey. Now, the thought made him shudder a bit.

Eddie had always figured she was so horny

because she was as into him as he was into her, but now he wasn't so sure. It was in her nature to be that way. If she could sleep with any random person who had the right amount of cash, then fucking him was nothing. Now that he thought about it, sometimes afterward, she seemed like she wasn't there, like her mind had retreated and she was just spacing out.

A tactic she'd learned as a prostitute, maybe? Release the mind from the body so her sanity remains intact?

The air in his room was stale, heavy with the breath of past tenants. A hot shower seemed just what he needed, so he ran the water to let it heat up and stripped down.

He sat on the toilet and studied his face in the mirror. Deep lines ran along his forehead, down from his nose to the corners of his mouth like knife wounds. Sharp daggers of facial hair sprouted over his cheeks, and he dragged a hand over them and inhaled the steam that began to creep from the shower.

Ten abortions? And she wonders why she can't get pregnant now?

Hot rage boiled within his belly, and it took every ounce of willpower for him not to pick up his phone and empty that rage into his wife's ear.

Stop it, Eddie. It's not her fault, and you know it.

Yeah, he thought. *That's right. Not her fault. She's a wonderful woman, a gorgeous, loving wife who loves you and cherishes you. Don't fuck this up. Don't you dare fuck this up!*

He stepped into the shower and let the scalding water burn away the day's filth. His thoughts went to Suzey's grandmother. Images of a withered old witch with sagging bags of flesh hanging from her decrepit body were formed in his mind. He saw little Suzey curled into a ball while the hunched-over hag beat her with a walking cane. It was this woman, he knew, who was the cause for all this, who was to blame for the life Suzey had chosen to pursue.

And all over some stupid fucking stork story?

He'd heard the story, of course—who hadn't? A tale told to kids so parents wouldn't have to explain the uncomfortable subject of sex and birth. Where do babies come from? Why, a great white bird brings them in a sling. Just swoops into the window of the nursery and plops the little darling right into its crib.

Did the old woman truly believe this shit? Or was she using a children's tale to get inside Suzey's head, pronouncing her to be evil with some sort of Dr. Seuss limerick?

Of course she would be fucked up, Eddie thought. *She witnesses her mother being murdered, then gets tortured by her bat-shit crazy grandmother for years.*

A deep guilt began to take shape in Eddie's head that made him want nothing more than to hear his wife's voice. For someone to go through all of that and make it out alive, then have a heart as big as Suzey's, was truly a miracle. The woman deserved to be pampered for the rest of her life.

When they'd first met, Suzey mentioned that she didn't think she wanted children, didn't think she would make a good mother. But Eddie persuaded her, told her he always imagined himself as a father—a family man. She seemed apprehensive about it but promised she would keep an open mind. *Let's just play it by ear,* she'd said.

When they'd found out she was pregnant the first time, they had only been dating for about eight months, but nonetheless, Eddie was excited. This woman was it for him, he knew that, and soon after the news, he proposed, and she accepted.

And then the baby died. So they tried again—the baby died. Third time's a charm?

No, another dead baby.

But he had a good feeling about this one—the new life in his wife's belly. Something told him everything was going to turn out great, that their luck was going to change.

And with this new account we bagged today, I'm expecting a nice big check.

He already knew he was going to use the money to build a nursery for their bundle of joy.

He cut the shower off and blew the excess water from his lips. With this new knowledge of Suzey's past seething in the center of his skull like a pulsating brain tumor, he felt it was his duty to help her find closure of some kind. As she'd told him the horrors of her past, the haunted look in her eyes unnerved him, and it pained him to see her this way.

Her grandmother.

Suzey had said it herself: she had no idea if the woman was alive or dead. Maybe if Eddie looked into it and found she was dead, it would exorcize some of Suzey's inner demons. They could visit her grave, show the old bitch what a great woman Suzey turned out to be, what a great life she was living now.

It's the least I can do.

He toweled off and plucked his phone from his discarded khakis, then dialed the number to his newly appointed secretary.

"H-hello?"

"Hey, Paula. Did I wake you?"

"N-no… no, Mr. Buddinger. Of course not."

"Great. I need your help."

Losing My Mind

Suzey sat in the living room slicing open boxes with a razor blade. The first box was full of framed photographs, mostly of her and Eddie in various smiley poses, but also a good amount of Eddie's family.

She stared at the picture of his sister Anne with her husband and two boys, their faces all lip, tooth, and gums as they beamed at the camera. Suzey imagined her and Eddie striking the same pose someday, their baby wedged snugly between them.

Beneath that was a strip of four photos that Suzey and Eddie had taken in a picture booth at the local fair the first year they'd met. It was only a week later when she'd found out she was pregnant for the first time. She would never forget the joy that lit up Eddie's face the day she told him, and it was then she really knew she loved him.

Suzey giggled as she eyed the photo strip, each image getting sillier as they went along. The bottom and final picture was of them kissing, their lips outstretched and tight like two woodpecker beaks.

She set the strip down, laughed again, and then reached in for the next one.

The glass broke as she tossed the frame away with a harsh gasp that swooshed from her stomach. The old woman's face had leered up at her, the corners of her mouth hanging with her loose jowls. Her eyes had a narrow squint, with gleaming hatred seeping from the dark slits. And the picture frame itself had been lined with white feathers, wet and misshapen as if they'd been floating in an oil spill.

Suzey stood and peered into the box just in case anything else was planning on jumping out at her, but there were only stacks of frames filled with smiling faces. Her eyes rolled to the mess of glass shards, the frame lying face-down.

It can't be... it's not real.

There were no existing photos of her grandma at her old home—as far as Suzey could remember—and even if there were, there was no way in hell Suzey would have kept one.

I'm losing my mind, she thought. *I've finally lost it. Finally gone insane.*

She tiptoed around the glass, concentrating to keep her walk steady as her knees wobbled beneath her and her stomach spun. Her toe nudged the edge of the frame, testing it to see if it was real. Fear coursed through her body as if the frame itself would bite her.

Stop being an idiot.

She forced herself to pick it up, and when she felt the soft frame border brush against her palm, a scream trumpeted from her mouth. She spun the frame, ready to throw it again, ready to scream again.

But she only laughed.

Eddie's grandmother, now deceased, smiled up at her. The woman's smile took up half of her face, reached up and nearly touched her eyes. A very pretty lady and, from what Eddie had told her, as sweet as peach cobbler.

The frame was bordered with a white satin fabric that made the old woman's face seem to glow. And now Suzey had broken it. She hoped it wasn't sentimental to Eddie in any way.

Get it together, Suzey.

As she swept up the mess, she couldn't keep from glancing at the photo of the old woman again and again, expecting her grandma's feral scowl to return. Since telling Eddie about her past, memories of her grandma swirled around in her head—things she'd either forgotten or subconsciously forced herself to bury away.

The beatings… the words… the stories.

She had the glass shards piled into a dustpan, but as she tried to stand, a needle of pain pierced her left temple and drove all the way through to the right side. Her teeth gnashed together as the agony increased, and she grabbed handfuls of her hair and bellowed at the ceiling. The glass rained from the dustpan to the floor as she collapsed backward and slammed her head against the hardwood.

And then the images flowed freely in her mind, as if whatever trunk the suppressed memories had been stored in was blown open. She writhed as they came, like ghosts with porcupine quills rolling around in her head, stabbing the memories back into her consciousness.

She saw her mother's murder, saw her brains splash against the wall and roll down in clumps. Saw the man unzip his blue jeans before entering the exit wound.

Bile stung her mouth and nose, and she sat up, wincing as the pain in her head seized her again.

She saw the repeated beatings, her grandmother whipping the electrical cord over Suzey's tiny, quivering body, screaming about evil and storks.

She saw all the men she'd been with, grunting and sweating above her, kissing and licking and sniffing and biting.

She saw the doctors killing the life inside of her. Again and again and again.

Some of these things she knew she'd done, knew she'd lived through, but the details of them had been blurry at best—but not now. Now they played in her mind like high-definition videos. All she could do was run from the room and dive into her bed where she could sob into her pillow.

She pulled her phone from her pocket and saw that Eddie still hadn't called. Her fingers punched in his number before she pressed the phone to her head hard enough to make the side of her face ache.

No answer.

He's left me. The weight of what I told him finally set in, and he realized he couldn't stay married to a whore.

She dialed again—no answer. The sound of his voicemail sent tremors of rage through her and she flung the phone at the wall, shattering it.

"Fuck!"

Her grandma's face once again swam into her mind, and she punched the wall, then with the other fist—over and over again. Bloody streaks painted the caved-in sheetrock.

"You stupid old cunt! I hope you're alive. I hope you're alive so I can cut out your fucking heart and shove it down your throat!"

Evil little bitch. Soulless. Satan's spawn.

"No… no, no, no!"

A twitch in her stomach. It stopped her dead in her tracks, and she sat on the edge of the bed, rubbing her midsection lovingly.

"I'm sorry, baby. So… so sorry. Mommy's calm, mommy's fine, mommy's—"

Another stab of pain, another memory. Something that couldn't be, something she knew was a lie. Her mind was toying with her, playing tricks on her now, just like with the photograph. This couldn't be real, couldn't be true.

Evil. An abomination.

Her hand went down to her groin, then to her stomach. Tears flowed from her eyes like they were open wounds.

My babies… my precious babies.
I am evil. I am soulless.

LAST LAUGH

"That's great news, Paula. I owe you big." Eddie paced the hotel room in his underwear and socks. "Why don't you take your husband out to a nice restaurant, huh? Any place you like."

"Thank you, Mr. Buddinger," Paula said through the phone. "It was no problem, really. She was the only Bastion in Travis. Easy to find in such a small town."

"And which cemetery did you say it was?"

"Saint Ignatius Memorial. I have the address written down."

Eddie sat on his bed and scribbled down the address on the back of a receipt. He stared at it for a moment, wondering if this was the right thing to do, if he should be sticking his nose in all this shit.

"Mr. Buddinger?"

"Oh, yes, sorry. That'll do, Paula. Thank you again. And remember, any place you like, okay?"

"Yes, sir. Thank you."

He hung up and immediately dialed Suzey's number. After coming up with his plan last night, he'd forgotten to call her. Now he could only hope she wasn't upset, wasn't letting her mind create unnecessary worry or jealousy.

No answer.

It went straight to voicemail, which wasn't like her. He dialed again, just to make sure, but got the same outcome.

The cab would be by the hotel to pick him up in half an hour to take him to the airport, then it was straight home with no layovers. He figured he could be at the house in four hours or so, which seemed like an eternity right then.

After telling me about her past, I'm sure she's on edge.

He knew she was. How could she not be?

She would be seething with worry, probably thinking Eddie was having second thoughts or running away or something like that. Suzey was always thinking the worst, always blowing things out of proportion. He could only hope that she didn't do anything drastic, that maybe her head was so clouded with anxiety she'd just forgotten to charge her phone.

Just get your ass home. As fast as you can.

He imagined the look on her face once he gave her the news. A smile dripping with relief.

After everything that happened to you, baby, all the shit you had to wade through, it's you who will have the last laugh in the end.

And together, we can spit on that hag's fucking grave.

SHARP LICKS OF PAIN

"It's your fault… all your fault!" Suzey's hand shook as she held the photo inches from her face, the old woman staring right back, a smug grin stretching her cheeks. "I'll k-kill you. I'll fucking *kill you!*"

The small rectangular box lay open beside her—the box she'd forgotten about. She didn't remember filling it, didn't remember packing it up and bringing it to their new home. The contents of that box confirmed what she'd known all along, confirmed what Grandma had drilled into her brain for so many years.

I'm evil. The stork never brought me a soul.

But Suzey still blamed Grandma, still resented her for showing her the truth.

Or maybe I could have been saved, she thought. *If you would have loved me and nurtured me, maybe things wouldn't have to be this way.*

She reached past the metal rods in the box and pulled out the book. Bloody fingerprints stained the cover and some of the pages were matted together with gore, but Suzey ignored all that and cracked it open.

She read the first line.

"On the last house in a little village, the storks had built a nest. And the mother stork sat in it with her four young ones who stretched out their necks and pointed their black beaks which had not yet turned red like those of the parent birds."

Suzey recited the words through clenched teeth, her molars grinding together. The pages rustled as she trembled.

And then the old woman's picture was back in her hand, the book on the floor in front of her. She didn't remember setting the book down, didn't remember picking the photo back up. The jagged glass bit into the tips of her fingers, but she only gripped it harder.

I know where you live. I know exactly where you live. And I think it's time the devil's spawn paid you a long overdue visit.

The next thing Suzey knew, she was on her feet, glass cracking and biting into her soles. She blinked and found herself at the front door.

Visions of electrical cords slicing through the air whipped her mind, the sharp licks of pain striping her body, breaking her skin. The taste of her screams filled her mouth, coated with tears and mucus and hopelessness.

Another sensation overtook her, nearly dropping her to her knees: the feel of cold metal entering her. Deep, further and further, deflating the life that grew there. In and out, in and out—over and over and over again.

And then she was outside, the hot sun assaulting her with its rays, drying the blood on her hands. Her aching fingers gripped something, and she looked down to find the electrical cord swinging from her grasp, wrapped tightly around her fist and turning the knuckles white.

Where did that come from?

With her free hand, Suzey fondled her belly as she traipsed down the driveway.

And then she was at Grandma's house. Her lip curled and she snarled as she stared at the front door, knowing the woman who tortured her as a child lay comfortably inside.

I'm home, Grandma. Finally home. And I have a story to tell you.

SUCH A SWEET OLD LADY

Eddie walked down the aisle until he reached his seat—a window seat, thank God—and shoved his carry-on into the overhead bin. He sidestepped his way to his chair, squeezing past an elderly woman who sat in the aisle seat. She turned toward him and smiled as he settled in.

"Always nice to have a handsome young man beside me," she said, then reached out and patted his knee.

"Not as nice as sharing knee space with such a stunning lady," Eddie said through a forced smile. "If I was only ten years younger…"

She giggled and put a hand to her chest. "Young man, behave yourself."

They smiled at each other for another couple of seconds before Eddie turned to the window and watched the men below load up the luggage.

"Going home or leaving home, dear?"

This is going to be a long flight, he thought. *Looks like a nap is out of the question.*

"Going home. To a pregnant wife, actually."

"Oh, how lovely. I'm sure she's very pretty."

Eddie couldn't help but sense the disappointment in her tone.

"Most beautiful woman on this planet."

"Mm-hmm." She suddenly found the in-flight magazines to be quite interesting, plucking one from the seat pocket in front of her and flipping through it.

Thank God.

Eddie turned back to the window and leaned his head against it, but just as his eyelids began to shut, a vibration tickled his thigh.

Hoping it was Suzey, he jammed his hand into his pocket and pulled out his phone. But it was only an email from Paula with a message: *'Thought you'd like to see this. Who was this lady anyway?'*

Eddie's brow creased as he opened the email and found a news article from the local paper in Travis: ELDERLY WOMAN FOUND MURDERED INSIDE OF HER HOME.

He checked the date, blinked, then double-checked it. Eleven years ago. A picture of the old woman sat in a floating box above the article, her face expressionless without a hint of joy or happiness. She was all scowl, cold and hard.

Joyce Bastion, sixty-five years old, was found dead in her bedroom on Sunday evening when her neighbor noticed the smell coming from the woman's home. Multiple lacerations and blunt trauma to the head were said to be the cause of death.

Bastion, widow and mother to a deceased daughter, lived alone according to the neighbor.

"Always kept to herself, didn't leave the house much. I just don't know who would do something like this to such a sweet old lady."

Eddie let the phone slip from his sweaty

palm and clatter to the floor. His mouth dried up and he tried to swallow but couldn't conjure the saliva. The seat in front of him blurred as he lost himself in thought.

"You dropped your phone, dear. You—are you all right?"

He heard the voice, but didn't register that it was aimed at him until the fragile fingers touched his knee. His body flinched and the woman retracted her hand and gasped.

"I'm—I'm sorry. Yes, I'm fine, I'm fine." Eddie looked into her face and almost jumped again at the wrinkled skin, the pale eyes, the silver hair. "Just tired, that's all. Dead tired."

"Oh, I know all about tired, dear. You know, I once fell asleep while I was…"

As the woman jabbered on, Eddie stared back out of the window, manners forgotten, and wondered what in the world all of this could mean. A *ding* echoed across the cabin and the pilot began his speech.

When the plane finally rolled toward the runway, Eddie didn't know whether to be relieved or terrified.

STORK, STORK, FLY AWAY

There she was, in her chair. Rocking, rocking.

The television was on, a gameshow—spin the wheel, win a prize.

"I'm home," Suzey said.

The old woman leapt from her chair and turned to face her. "My God, missy. You scared me half to death."

"It's been a long time, but I'm finally home. You were right, you know. Right about everything."

Grandma tried to fake a smile, massaging

her hands as she took shuffling steps forward. "I don't mind you coming to visit me, missy, but a courtesy knock would be welcome next time."

"But you didn't have to treat me the way you did."

"I what?"

"You could have loved me… cared for me. Things didn't have to turn out this way, Grandma. You know? Maybe you could have helped me."

Suzey reached down and grabbed the other end of the cord. She snapped it between her fists, sending a deafening *crack* through the air.

"Now wait just a minute—"

"Stork, stork, fly away."

Whap!

The cord sliced through the air in a vicious arc that walloped the old woman on the side of the neck and down her shoulder. She gasped, moaned, and fell backward. Her backside made a loud *thud,* and she rocked herself as she gripped her hips with quivering hands.

"Stand not on one leg, I pray."

Whap!

A long red welt rose on Grandma's arm as the cord smacked it and wrapped itself around. Suzey ripped it away, baring her teeth.

"P-please… please stop." The hag's voice was weak and trembling, dripping with pain and fear. "Why are y-you—?"

"See your wife is in her nest, with her little ones at rest."

Suzey marched forward and kicked the underside of Grandma's waddle-like chin. The false teeth shattered and oozed from the old woman's mouth like broken eggshells, swimming in bloody saliva.

Grandma lay on her back, kicking her legs to try and scoot away from her attacker, but there wasn't enough strength to carry her far. A high-pitched whimper rattled lightly from her throat like helium escaping a balloon.

"Don't k-kill me. Don't—please d-don't—"

"They will hang one, and fry another." Suzey crushed the broken dentures beneath her feet as she pursued the old woman.

Trying to act innocent, trying to beg for mercy. The nerve… the fucking audacity of this woman.

"You take it—take w-whatever you want.

Just l-leave m-my home. Just leave me be—"

Whap! Whap! Whap!

Suzey screamed as her arm grew a mind of its own, a mind thirsty for blood and revenge. The cord flayed strips of flesh away from Grandma's face, arms, and chest. Skin opened, leaking blood onto the carpet.

The despicable hag had ceased all screaming, all begging, and curled into a protective ball—just the way Suzey used to do. The woman's bowels released and her bladder deflated, forming an odorous puddle around her pitiful body.

"They will shoot a third and roast his brother!" The pistol had been tucked into Suzey's waistline behind her back, and her hand reached around, grabbed hold of it, and pulled it free.

She didn't remember bringing it, but her hand knew it was there.

Grandma's white fluff of hair was soaked in red and yellow and brown, and Suzey buried the muzzle there, pressed down until she felt skull, and then pulled the trigger.

She stood there for a few minutes, watching the blood puddle grow and soak into the carpet. It reached the kitchen linoleum and skated across its surface.

Suzey leaned over and put her mouth right to the old woman's ear. "I'm evil after all, Grandma. No soul. An empty shell, just like you said. But not my baby."

She ran her fingertips over her belly and smiled.

"The stork will bring my baby a soul… I'll make him do it."

AND HER BABY SCREAMED

Suzey lay on her bed, hands blood-stained and shaking. Her thoughts were cloudy, muddy, and she couldn't put the pieces together.

She remembered finding the box, remembered the metal rods that lay within it, stained with old, dried blood that covered half the length of each one. But that box still lay on the living room floor, away from her.

My... my babies.

She couldn't look at the rods, didn't like the memories they summoned. And the book was there, caked with blood. Just seeing it, with the cartoon stork on the cover, caused the story to recite itself within her head. Non-stop, over and over.

She remembered finding Grandma. There was yelling, a possible struggle, but it could have all been a dream. She thought she remembered the sun on her skin, but she wasn't sure if she ever left the house.

But the blood. Where did all the blood come from?

A wave of panic set in as she bent over and peered toward the crotch of her pants—it was clean, no sign of trauma. A sigh of relief blew from her lips, and she allowed herself to sink backward into the bed, the down pillow squashing beneath her weight.

The broken glass. I just cut myself on the broken glass, that's all.

Her eyelids grew heavy and she was powerless to fight them as they lowered and sleep scraped away at her consciousness.

An old woman stood at the end of her bed, smiling at her, tossing torn bits of hot dog bun onto the sheets. Blood oozed from between her teeth and striped her chin before dripping to the floor. Red wounds like zebra stripes streaked across her flesh, seeping globs of thick blood like mouths spitting out chewed food.

"They're good luck, you know," the old woman said.

Suzey shot up to a sitting position, then scooted backward and kicked her comforter toward the bleeding woman. Balls of bread, soaked in blood, bounced off her body and face. "What are you—why are you here?"

"Greeks thought the stork was a baby thief, can you believe that?"

"Get out of my house… go. Leave!"

The windows blew open and crashed against the wall. Glass tinkled and rained to the floor, and a cloud of white feathers burst in, swirling until landing gently on Suzey's bed.

And then the stork entered. It stood on the windowsill with one foot, its neck stretching into the room as it pointed its long, red beak toward Suzey.

The white bird opened its mouth and hissed, extending its wings and flapping a whirlwind of hot air over Suzey's body that burned like car exhaust.

"Good luck… good luck…" The woman smiled and bled.

Sloppy mounds of bloody bread slapped Suzey in the face, piling up on the mattress. "No, no. Please no!"

The stork hopped into the room, its feathers soggy and hanging from its body—patches of gray skin showed through the tattered quills. When it flapped its wings again, the cries and whimpers of children filled the air. Their tortured, cherubic faces were pressed tightly against the stork's skin, screaming from beneath its flesh as if trying to escape from its stomach.

Its eyes glowed red, and as it strutted to the foot of the bed, its head bobbed back and forth atop its rubbery neck. The tall bird's wet, webbed feet slapped against the floor, soaking dirty pond water into the carpet.

"Baby thieves, missy." The old woman took hold of Suzey's ankles and spread them apart with unnatural power.

Suzey's joints popped, and she screamed. She tried to fight and kick the woman away but was powerless against her strength.

When Suzey's legs were pulled apart as far as they would go, a piercing wail exploded from her birth canal. It blew with such force that it swept the old woman off her feet and into the next room.

My baby!

The stork was unaffected and stood its ground, peering into her womanhood with a stretch of its neck.

Her baby cried, long and hard, and she thought she could feel it retreating deeper inside of her, trying to hide from the devil bird.

"Please…"

And then the beak was in her, digging deep, to her core, and her baby screamed.

GET HOME

When the plane finally landed after what felt like an eternity in the air, Eddie dialed Suzey's number before the captain said it was okay to do so.

Straight to voicemail again.

"Shit! Goddamnit!"

"You okay—?"

"Will you please leave me the fuck alone and mind your fucking business?!"

The woman gasped, stood, and turned her back to Eddie as the other passengers exchanged looks and shot glances his way.

He ignored them all and dialed 9-1-1.

"9-1-1 emergency, do you need police, fire, or an ambulance?"

"Police, police please! I need someone to do a welfare check on my wife. I've been calling and she won't answer and I think she may be in some kind of trouble."

The operator got the address and assured Eddie they would be at the house as soon as possible, but Eddie planned on beating them there.

Just as the 'Safe to Unbuckle Your Seatbelts' sign lit up, he forced his way through the crowd, leaving his carry-on behind, and exploded out of the plane.

Raised voices and curse words were fired in his direction from behind, but he pushed on, sprinted into the terminal, down the escalator, and through the doors.

"Emergency—I have an emergency!" he told the woman whose cab he had just confiscated. She stood outside with her arms in the air.

"Nice one, buddy," the cabbie said. "She looked like a snobby bitch anyway. Where to?"

Eddie shouted the address. "Please, man, as fast as you can. Huge tip for you, okay?

Go, go, go!"

"You got it, buddy."

And they peeled off, zooming around cars, and screeched onto the highway toward home.

Eddie didn't know what he'd do when he got there, didn't know what he'd say to his wife. He just knew he had to get home.

I'VE COME TO CLOUD THE WATER

Suzey awoke screaming and thrashing. Feathers floated all around her, coating the bed, and for a moment, she thought the stork was there, in her arms, fighting with her. But she saw that it was her pillow, torn open and spewing its innards.

Long, deep breaths inflated her lungs, and she wiped the sweat dripping from her face.

Jesus Christ… it felt so real.

She could still feel the stork's beak inside of her, tunneling, searching for her baby—a rhythmic throb pulsed between her legs. She winced, fell from her bed, and writhed on the floor.

The old woman… Why was she in my dream?

"Eddie?" No answer.

She didn't know how long she'd been asleep, and she knew he was due home sometime today. Her phone lay in pieces on the floor, and she cursed herself for breaking it, longing to hear her husband's voice.

Her eyes flew to the window, but it was shut tight. The image of the massive bird smashing into the room through that window still haunted her. The cries of the children vibrated through her flesh and refused to stop.

No, I won't let it have my baby.

"You can't have my fucking baby!"

Eddie's pistol lay on the end table by the bed, and she grabbed it, squeezed it. Bloody fingerprints dotted the handle, and she wondered where they came from for a moment, but then shooed the thoughts away as she tightened the laces on her running shoes.

The sun was still out, though the hottest part of the day had passed. In the distance, the pond water sparkled, and her eyes danced across the surface in search of her nemesis.

Can't have him… can't have my baby.

She launched from her doorstep in a full sprint, gun in hand. Heads swung in her direction, loud words were launched at her, but she ignored all of that. Joggers and dog walkers and people pushing strollers, every one of them parted, moving out of her way as if they comprehended the magnitude of her mission and understood what she had to do.

The lone duck floated happily in the center of the pond, dunking its head to cool off every few seconds. It swam in the opposite direction when Suzey came storming by, quacked to show its disapproval, and then finally took to the air.

It could sense my anger, Suzey thought. *Knows I've come to cloud the water with fowl blood.*

The elderly couple with the black labs walked by as Suzey stood at the edge of the pond, gun out in front of her, sweeping the water.

"What in the hell are you doing?" a male voice said. "We got kids around here, lady."

Suzey heard the words but didn't acknowledge them. She breathed deeply through her mouth as she searched but didn't see the bird anywhere.

"Did you hear me, goddammit? We're calling the cops."

Suzey swung the pistol around and aimed it at the couple. "Where is it?"

The woman screamed and fell to the ground, covering her head with her arms. The dogs barked, yanked on their leashes, and snapped their jaws.

"Calm down—just stay calm," the man said, gripping the leashes with one hand and holding out the other. He fell to his knees and said something softly to his wife.

Suzey growled, leaving the quivering couple behind as she jogged around the bend and searched the other side of the pond. She would find the son-of-a-bitch, she knew. If it took all fucking night, she would find him.

A horde of people stood in a tight huddle on the street, each one stretching their neck to get a look at something. Then Suzey saw the police cars, the ambulance. All parked in front of Mrs. Hopps' house. She hoped briefly that the woman was okay, but she just didn't have time to worry about it.

The sound of rustling feathers.

It came from her right, and her head

snapped in its direction. She crept toward it, gun at the ready.

Through the tall grass, there stood her enemy, stark white against the green of the pond water.

The stork stood on one leg, and as Suzey took a closer step, its neck uncurled and its head swiveled around to look at her.

From behind, she heard loud voices, baritone arguing.

The stork opened its wings.

Suzey fired.

White feathers blew into the air in a vast burst. The bird floated on the water, a red cloud forming beneath it.

Screams, shouts, angry voices behind her.

"Put the gun down, now!"

Suzey waded into the water, grabbed the stork by the neck, and hauled it out. As she strode back to the edge of the pond—her prize dangling heavily from her left hand, the gun held tight in her right—she saw the police officers and realized they were yelling at her, every one of them with a gun pointed, faces full of hate and sweat.

"Put it down!"

"I have to save my baby," she said. "I have to."

And then she was running. She didn't remember taking off, but she could hear the pursuing footsteps behind her.

Her house was just down the street—almost there. The stork's body dragged along, trailing blood, water, and feathers.

At her front door now. Demands were screamed at her, and she spun around and fired at them without thought.

"I have to save my baby!"

She jumped into the house, slammed the door behind her, and locked it.

The vibrations from the slamming door rang through the air, and Suzey's legs grew wobbly, her vision darkening. She tried to concentrate, tried to brace herself against the wall before she fell over, but she found herself on the floor before she even knew what had happened.

Blood pooled around her knees, and it confused her.

The stork's blood.

She tried to think about Eddie, her loving and understanding husband, the warmth of his embrace and the strength of his arms around her.

Where is he? she thought. *Where is my love?*

STORK

Her fingernails raked across the hardwood floor as she crawled toward their bedroom.

A nap… I just need a nap. I'm so tired.

She thought about their baby, how happy they would be once he or she was born. They would be a family then, just the three of them. They could live happily ever after. It wouldn't matter anymore that she had no soul, wouldn't matter that she was evil. Eddie and their child could help her, could make things right.

But the darkness engulfing her grew stronger, and before she could make it to the bedroom door, it swallowed her whole.

AS DEEP AS IT COULD GO

The cab screeched around the turn, and the driver slammed on the brakes. Blue and red lights flashed all around, and the street was thick with police cruisers.

"Oh God—oh Jesus." Eddie kicked the door open and began a slow walk toward his home.

"Hey, buddy. Where the hell you going?"

Eddie pulled out his wallet, flung all the cash he had into the passenger window, then weaved his way through the cars.

A congregation of police stood at the end of his driveway, along with an ambulance. Two medics loaded an officer onto a stretcher, the man's uniform torn open and a bloody bandage strapped to his chest.

"Whoa, sir. This area is closed off." A large officer with thick arms shoved Eddie backward.

"That's—that's my house. What's h-happening?"

The officer's eyes widened. "You better come with me, sir."

Eddie was led to the group of police at his driveway, all cursing at one another and glancing at the house every few seconds. An older man in a white button-up and khakis glanced over at Eddie and the large officer as they approached.

"Sir, this man says he lives here."

"Yes, that's my house. My pregnant wife is—oh God, where is she? Where's Suzey?!"

The officers all exchanged looks, and from what Eddie could tell, the news wasn't good.

"You say your wife's pregnant?" the older officer asked.

"Yes, that's right. Where the fuck is she?!"

Eddie peered toward his home. He saw the

blood on the front patio, the smears of it across the door and handle—he saw the bullet holes.

Falling to his knees, he grimaced at the bolts of pain that shot through his legs when they hit the pavement. "Please tell me what's going on."

"Sir, your wife shot a police officer. She was seen at the pond there with the gun, shooting at birds and threatening neighbors." The cop ran his hand over his face, exchanging more looks with the others. "And I have reason to believe she may be involved in a murder."

How could he know that? It had happened eleven years ago. It's impossible…

"An old woman who lives just down the street, on the other side of the pond there, was found dead today, bullet to the head. I'm willing to bet the bullet we pull out of my officer's chest will match it."

Eddie again studied the blood on the door, the holes. "You didn't… kill her, did you?"

"Shots were fired, but she made it into the house on her own and locked the door behind her. We've been trying to reason with her but can't get a response."

Eddie wiped the tears from his face. "I'll go in and talk to her, okay? Please. You all stay out here, let me talk to my wife."

Words were exchanged as the men talked it over, but Eddie was in no mood to wait. He stormed toward the house, ignoring the shouts behind him. His key slid into the door, the handle slick with blood, and he entered the home with a sinking feeling in his stomach.

"Suzey! Baby, where are you?!"

A trail of blood was smeared across the floor, leading into the bedroom. And feathers. White feathers everywhere.

He wanted to run into the room, but his legs wouldn't let him. So he crept along, eyes glued to the bloody slug trail beneath him. Sitting on the floor amongst shards of broken glass, just outside of the bedroom, was a box. Its flaps lay open, bloody smudges along the edges.

Eddie didn't recognize it—he knelt down and peered inside. A children's book lay on top, a cartoon rendering of a stork in flight on the cover. He tossed that aside, crinkling his brow at what was lying beneath it.

Long metal rods, each one coated and rusted with dried blood. He picked one up and ran his finger along the shaft—nearly the entire length was painted with blood. He grabbed them all, counting three total.

No… no, it's not what you think.

"Suzey! Suzey, answer me!" He was standing again, easing the bedroom door open.

A low moaning sound, almost a growl, and a repetitive thumping.

When he entered the room, when his eyes fell onto the bed, he collapsed backward, shaking his head in shock.

"Suzey, no. S-stop—what are you…?" Eddie raked his nails down his cheeks. "Oh God…"

His wife lay on her back, feet propped up on the edge of the bed so her knees were bent and pointing to the ceiling. Her legs were spread wide, her panties on the floor.

She clutched the dead stork by the base of its neck, and with violent thrusts, shoved its beak and head into herself—as deep as it could go.

Eddie forced himself back to his feet and approached the bed with hot tears rushing from his eyes. A leaking hole on Suzey's chest spewed blood in bursts, soaking into the mattress. More blood oozed from her birth canal as the stork's head was shoved in again, the bird's feathers soaking and dripping with red.

The gun lay just beside her, and with a shaking hand, Eddie picked it up. He lay next to his wife, next to his child. His family.

"I love you, baby. I'll always love you."

He reached down and found her hand, intertwined his fingers with hers, squeezing tight. The gun's barrel entered his mouth.

Suzey turned her head and smiled at him. "I love you too." Her hand went limp in his, her eyes and mouth remaining open.

Eddie whimpered once and then pulled the trigger.

I'M ON MY—

—a short story—

Morris wanted to scream as he walked from the office building toward his Camry, but he breathed instead, holding his composure.

Ten years. Ten years he'd been working for that company, and it was finally paying off.

I've been their best guy since day one. It's about time.

When they had brought him into the office, he was sure it was bad news. Not because he had done anything to warrant any kind of reprimand, but because he was pessimistic by nature.

And he had never seen his bosses call anyone into their office for anything good.

"Morris," Mr. Whitehead had started. "You know I like you. You know I think you're a good worker, right?"

Morris had nearly passed out right then and there. He couldn't lose his job. Not now. Not with a baby in Melissa's belly. Not while they were waiting to hear back to see if their offer on the house was accepted.

"Y-yes, sir." He'd wanted to say more, but his words sizzled away on his tongue like water on a hot griddle.

"Stand up," Mr. Whitehead had said.

Morris did.

Then the scowl on his boss' face curled into a grin, his smoker's teeth like sallow toenails past his pasty lips, and he reached out his hand. "Welcome to upper management, Morris. You earned it, you son-of-a-bitch."

Morris had to clench his teeth to keep himself from squealing as he gripped Mr. Whitehead's hand, which was as soft as a cinder block. His boss, who was usually devoid of all emotion, pulled him in and hugged him. He smelled like cheap cologne and stale cigarette smoke, and Morris held his breath as they took turns patting each other on the back.

There had been an awkward five minutes or so after the strange embrace they had shared, and then Mr. Whitehead told Morris to head home for the day, that he deserved a three-day weekend.

"Come Monday, get ready for some real work. Yeah?"

"Of course, sir. I'm—"

"No more of that *sir* bullshit, all right? It's Abe from now on. You're the new *sir* around these parts." He cackled, coughed—spat something into a crumpled napkin that had been sitting on his desk beside a photo of him and his dog—and then excused Morris.

Morris hopped into his car and slammed the door. He stared at himself in the rearview—a pair of baby blue, miniature sneakers hung from the mirror, and he held them in the palm of his hand for a moment as his eyes welled up with tears.

Getting a promotion didn't make them rich, but it sure helped. No more worrying about the upcoming hospital bill. No more worrying about being able to afford their house payment—if their offer was accepted. Melissa could stop freaking out about missing so much work while she recovered from the delivery. He could feel the stress melting off him like candle wax.

One day, babycakes, he thought, *you won't have to work at all.*

He wiped his eyes with the heel of his palm, then pulled his phone from his pocket.

Melissa's name was at the top of the list in his text messages—though it was labeled BABYCAKES—and he started typing, grinning as his thumbs tapped the screen. They hardly ever talked on the phone anymore. It was always text messages now, like little virtual love letters.

MORRIS: Huge news today! Got cut loose early. Get ready to celebrate!

It took less than a minute to get a reply.

BABYCAKES: Don't mess with me!!! What is it????

MORRIS: ;-)

BABYCAKES: Evil bastard!!! Well hurry home!!! I luv u

MORRIS: Luv u 2

They'd been talking about the promotion for years, and Melissa was always the optimistic one. Telling him not to worry about it, to just keep working hard, that it would pay off eventually. Morris had been on the verge of quitting multiple times, but she talked him out of it, told him to hang in there and not let his years of hard work be all for nothing.

And now, when it mattered most, it actually happened.

Holy shit!

As he pulled out of the parking lot, he threw in Melissa's Black Eyed Peas album, then switched it over to "I Gotta Feeling." He always hated the group, especially hated that fucking song, but it was Melissa's favorite, and whenever she was in a particularly good mood, she blasted it, nodding her head and waving her arms, shoving Morris to get him to join in.

Right at that moment, the song felt appropriate, and he smiled as he nodded to the beat and pulled out of the parking lot.

* * *

The deluxe sushi platter from Uchiko, a bottle of Crios Rosé, and a bunch of peach-colored roses sat in the passenger seat—each one Melissa's favorite. Two of which pregnant women weren't supposed to touch, but even their doctor had smirked at this myth.

"If that were true, there'd be no French or Japanese people walking around, right?" the doctor had said as she slathered Melissa's stomach in petroleum jelly.

Besides, he thought. *It's a special occasion. A few mouthfuls of alcohol and mercury never hurt nobody.*

Since leaving work, a couple hours had passed, and his phone had been blowing up with text messages. He hadn't expected it to take so long, but Uchiko was packed, and it took forty-five minutes just to get his to-go platter. Not to mention Central Foods, where he'd picked up the wine and flowers, was swarming with customers, the lines filing back into the aisles.

But none of that could spoil Morris' mood. He'd just smiled and waited patiently while sending generic replies to his wife as the texts kept rolling in.

BABYCAKES: OMG! Where are you already!?!?

MORRIS: Be home soon, babe

BABYCAKES: Seriously, this is so WRONG!

MORRIS: Luv u!

I'M ON MY—

BABYCAKES: I want a divorce!!!
MORRIS: Kisses! Muah!

He knew she was probably pissed for real by now, but the second she saw what he'd be bringing, the second he told her what it was they were celebrating, all anger would disintegrate.

Morris had heard warnings from just about every person he knew—even some he didn't— about how Melissa's hormones would turn her into some kind of foul-mouthed monster, and that he shouldn't take anything mean she might say to heart during her pregnancy because it wasn't really her speaking.

None of that happened. She was a little more tired than usual, but that was all. Hell, her sex drive had even intensified since the pregnancy, and Morris wasn't the kind of guy who got weirded out by her bulging belly. They'd had some of the best sex of their entire relationship in the last nine months.

As he grew closer and closer to their apartment complex, his stomach started to churn, his palms grew sweaty, and his mouth dried up. He couldn't wait to see the look on her face when he told her, couldn't wait to hear that *eeeeeee* noise she always made when she got excited.

His cell vibrated again, and he chuckled as he pulled the phone from the cup holder and glanced at the screen.

BABYCAKES: I'm pretty sure I hate you. WHERE THE HELL R U???!!!

MORRIS: I'm on my—

Something smacked the front bumper hard, throwing Morris' forehead into the steering wheel. His phone flew from his hand at the same time something collided with the windshield, bashing it inward and frosting the glass with cracks.

As he slammed his foot against the brake pedal, there was a scraping and squealing sound coming from underneath the car as he dragged whatever it was the last twenty yards or so.

Morris threw the car into park, then cupped his face and moaned in pain. The gash on his forehead spewed streams of blood that ran down the sides of his nose and dripped into his eyes—it sucked into his nostrils with every breath.

Raw fish strips, broken glass, and rose petals lay on the floor in a puddle of sizzling wine.

The taste at the back of his throat made Morris gag and cough as he threw his car door open and let himself fall out onto the concrete.

The car hissed and clicked. The scent and flavor of burning oil stung his nose and throat.

A deer, he thought. *I hit a fucking deer.*

No. Not a deer. Not unless this was some kind of circus deer that had learned to ride a bicycle.

Morris forced himself to his feet, wincing at the searing pain in his face and chest. A diagonal stripe of agony burned over his torso where the seatbelt had gone taut.

But none of the pain mattered as he stared at the mangled bicycle sitting crooked and bent on the hood of his Camry.

The seat and handlebars were planted into the windshield. The back wheel, though slightly bent, spun in place, the metal spokes stained red with blood.

"Oh—oh, Jesus…" Morris dropped to his hands and knees, praying he would see another pair of eyes staring back at him. Quivering with pain maybe, but open, with life behind them.

"H-hello? Are you—?"

A hand lay just in front of him. Small, three of the fingers broken, the shredded skin revealing the meat and bone beneath. Instead of a pain-stricken face, he saw the back of a head, the hair matted with blood.

"No—nononono."

Morris jumped back to his feet, launched himself into the car, and searched for his phone. His hands shook so badly that when he finally grabbed it, he accidentally tossed it to the back seat.

And then he stopped.

He took a deep breath. Glanced at his reflection in the rearview before quickly looking away.

Check on the kid first. If he's alive, I'll call an ambulance, police. Anybody who can help him.

And if he's not?

Morris stepped back into the street, dropped to his stomach, and grabbed the kid's wrist. He expected some kind of reaction when he grabbed at the hand, but it remained limp—not a sound from the twisted child beneath his Camry.

He'd heard somewhere that you're not supposed to move a person after an accident. That they're supposed to stay exactly how they were until medically trained personnel arrived on scene. But Morris pulled on the tiny arm anyway.

He figured the body would be trapped, caught up on the undercarriage or something. But it slid out easily, making a harsh scraping sound as it was dragged across the rough concrete, smearing blood across the blacktop.

A boy. Maybe seven years old.

One look at his face and Morris dropped the boy's arm, turned his head, and splashed hot vomit over the street.

He looked around and didn't see anyone—no sign of the boy's parents.

What the fuck were you doing out here in the dark, goddammit?!

The boy's eyes were closed. His forehead had been ripped from his skull and hung to the side like a flap of bloody leather. His shirt was so soaked with blood that Morris was too scared to look under the fabric to see the damage.

This kid was dead. He was alive five

minutes ago, most likely walking his bike—since his body ended up under the car. A flat tire, maybe, or a busted chain. He was probably in a rush to get home to his mom and dad because it was already dark and he knew he was going to be in trouble for being late.

And now he was dead. He was dead because of Morris.

And there's not a fucking thing anyone can do about that now.

Morris checked over his shoulder, rose to his feet and spun, making sure nobody was around, that nobody saw what happened.

As quickly as he could, he popped the trunk, lifted the boy, and gently placed his body inside. He would have to clean up the blood later, he knew, but right then, he had to act fast. Get the hell out of there before someone drove by or the boy's parents came calling for him.

It took a few minutes to yank the bicycle free, but he got it and forced it into his back seat. He didn't hit the gas too hard—didn't want to peel out and alert anyone—and he left the scene as quickly and quietly as possible.

He's already dead. I didn't mean to kill him. He shouldn't have been messing around out here at night like that! No reason to throw my life away. Not now. Not when everything is finally going right. Melissa and the baby... they need me.

And I'd do anything for them.

* * *

"You okay, sir?"

"I'm fine. Just had a... a little accident. No big deal." Morris had forgotten about his own injuries, and he forced a smile as the teenage girl glared at him from behind the checkout counter. He slid his palm over his forehead, chuckled, and wiped the blood on his pant leg.

"That'll be eleven thirty-nine, sir." She took the money, then frowned again. "You sure you're okay? That looks pretty deep."

"It's nothing. Really."

Morris took the shovel from the counter and tried not to look too suspicious as he walked out of the store.

* * *

BABYCAKES: Okay... I've gone from pissed off to scared. Are you okay?! Tell me what's going on please!!! Or I'm calling the police. I'm not kidding, Morris!!!

MORRIS: I'm fine, babycakes. I didn't mean to worry you, just wanted to surprise you. I'll be home soon. I love you, Melissa. I love you so much. I don't know what I'd do without you

Morris turned off the phone and shoved it into his pocket. Before that message, there'd been ten others, all unanswered. He knew Melissa was probably losing her damn mind by now, and he'd have to think up one hell of a story to get out of this mess.

The hole took much longer to dig than he'd anticipated. It had been a dry summer, and they were in the middle of a record-breaking drought. The dirt was as hard as concrete, and by the time he had the hole as deep and wide as he wanted, his arms and shoulders felt like they'd been ripped free from his torso.

He tossed the shovel away and wiped the sweat from his face with the back of his forearm. Each breath wheezed out of his barren throat as he trudged toward the car and popped the trunk.

I'M ON MY—

Just a boy.

Tears filled Morris' eyes, raining down on the body—he couldn't help but imagine the boy as his own son.

What would I do if someone did this to my child?

Killing the kid and then taking him away like this—the parents would never get closure. They would assume their boy was kidnapped. Would probably be on the news, begging whoever took their son to please bring him back, that they love him so much and would do anything to have him back in their loving arms.

"I'm so sorry. I'm s-so fucking sorry…"

He scooped up the crooked body into his arms and slowly made his way toward the freshly dug grave. He'd made sure to make it large enough to fit both the boy and the bicycle.

Once the body and bike were inside the hole, Morris collapsed to the dirt beside it. He glared down at the boy whose face was pointed toward the night sky where the full moon shone like God's judging eye.

"If you would have been alive, I would have gotten you help. I swear to God I would have. But you understand, don't you? I have a family to take care of. My own son coming into the world any day now. They *need* me." Morris wiped the tears away, then climbed down into the hole with the boy, gripped his small hand, and ran his thumbs over the knuckles. "I wish I knew your name. If I knew your name, I'd give it to my son. I would. To honor you. I—"

The boy coughed once. It was weak and barely noticeable, but it was a cough for sure. His eyes fluttered open, and within the next few seconds, his bloody face twisted into a grimace as he began to cry. Asking for his mother. The cries became screams as his squinted eyes locked onto Morris.

Morris pulled himself out of the grave before kicking his feet and scooting away from it. His head shook from side to side as chaotic thoughts ripped through his mind.

Alive—he's alive… Oh Jesus Christ he's alive!

Morris covered his ears and bared his teeth as the boy continued to bawl, begging for help, going on and on about how much it hurt.

I'm going to help him now, just like I said I was. He's alive, he can live through this. He needs an ambulance.

I'M ON MY—

But instead of reaching into his pocket for his phone, Morris walked toward the shovel, picked it up, and twisted his hands over the wooden handle, ignoring the splinters stabbing his palms.

He hopped back into the hole. Raised the shovel over his head.

Even as the boy screamed and pleaded, it was Melissa's laugh Morris heard in his mind.

Her moans of pleasure when they made love. The way she said *eeeeeee* when she was excited.   It was the cry of his newborn baby boy.

"I'm sorry," Morris said, then swung the shovel down. Then again. And again and again and again. "My family needs me."

And I'd do anything for them.

THE END

A NEW FATHER

Shane McKenzie
—September 3, 2024—

Okay, so I know both those stories were pretty fucking heavy. And I paired them for a reason. Allow me to explain!

When I came up with the idea for *Stork*, my wife was pregnant with our first child. And when the idea presented itself, the fact that I could even have such dark thoughts at a time like that was troubling to me. But looking back on it, it's obvious that I was terrified and confused—who wouldn't be, right?!

We had no idea what we were doing, and because we were new to the idea of being parents—not to mention ignorant as fuck—we read every book, took tons of classes, and worst of all, listened to the advice of friends and family. Why is it that everything they had to say about parenthood always started with, "Oh, just wait till…"

I started reading *What to Expect When You're Expecting*, and realized about a quarter of the way through it that it was just listing, in detail, every single fucking thing that could possibly go wrong.

I remember we took a class on natural birth, because we had it in our heads that an epidural would harm and drug our baby (Spoiler Alert: my wife ABSOLUTELY got an epidural because—I know this is shocking news—giving birth FUCKING HURTS!). The class was way more spiritual than we'd anticipated. I'm laughing as I type this, re-membering the moment we both realized we'd made a mistake.

The instructor had us all close our eyes and do 'om' chants as a group. She would tap this little gong, and then all together, we'd go, "Oooomm." So, I started to feel a bit ridiculous, and I cracked my eyes just to see if everyone was participating. And the only other person with their eyes open was my wife, and once we locked stares, it took everything we had to not laugh out loud.

Yeah, that was the last time we took that class. And I only got through half of *What to Expect When You're Expecting* before I came to the conclusion that it was freaking me out more than educating me.

But the psychological damage had already been done, and I spent just about every waking fucking moment scared and paranoid about all the things that could potentially go wrong, both in utero and during the actual childbirth.

And during this time, with my brain spinning and with every night filled with nightmares that seemed like they were written and directed by Lars von Trier, the idea for *Stork* just sort of popped into existence (along with another idea for a book called *Fairy* that I'll be releasing eventually).

The idea upset and disturbed me, so much so that I refused to write it until my daughter was born and I knew for certain that both my wife and child were safe and healthy.

And then right there in the hospital, with my wife asleep and my baby girl lying in her plastic crib at the foot of the bed, I finally wrote it. What you read in *Stork* is a young man expressing his fears of becoming a father, of starting a family.

Little did I know that the fears were only just beginning. The real fear started on the drive home from the hospital, with my brand new baby in the back, strapped into a car seat that I wasn't fully confident was installed properly. It was during that drive that I was reminded how dangerous driving a car is, and how every vehicle around you can potentially kill you.

That's what was going through my mind anyway, and by the time we got home, my hands were aching from the pressure of squeezing that damn steering wheel.

As time went on, my fears really only got worse. The whole world was just one danger after another, each one trying desperately to harm my family.

On top of all that irrationality, I was feeling the pressure of providing for them and giving them everything they wanted and needed, no matter what the cost.

Because the love I felt in my heart for my family was something I'd never experienced before. It's so fucking powerful that it changes you chemically, makes you realize that there's nothing you won't do to keep them safe.

And this is when the idea for the short story *I'm on My—* was born, among many others. In this story, our character is about to be a new father, and he's finally able to give his family everything he thinks they need. Before an accident threatens to take all that away from him. What would someone in this state of mind do, or wouldn't do, for the sake of his family?

I am writing this essay the day after my 42nd birthday. My wife and I have been together for 18 years now, married for 14, and we've got two amazing children. These days, I think about things much differently. See, I'm not great at many things. I can't fix or build anything, don't take care of myself the way I know I should, and don't know dick about maintaining cars or lawns. But there are two things I know for goddamn certain that I'm great at: being a husband and being a father.

But reading these stories allowed me to reunite with the young version of myself, full of fear for what the future might hold. Certain things may not have turned out exactly the way that younger Shane had hoped, but I think he'd be pretty fucking proud of what we've accomplished.

Now, let's switch gears quickly so I can introduce the excerpt of my upcoming novel *Monsters Don't Cry*.

While many of my stories come from deep psychological baggage, I'd say an equal amount of them come from my pure love of horror and the movies I grew up watching (not to say that each and every one of those aren't also packed with a plethora of my fears and experiences).

With *Monsters Don't Cry*, I thought, "What if I wrote a Beauty-and-the-Beast-esque love story, but with a slasher?"

Then I thought, "What if the slasher was like a female Jason Voorhees, big and nasty and violent as fuck?"

And then this insane, fucked up book just came pouring out of me. Now that I'm thinking about it, and after revisiting this book after so long, I can definitely see so many of my own insecurities front and center in these characters. Feeling less-than everyone around me, comparing myself to others, still trying to figure out where I fit and what my purpose was.

This is one of my personal favorites of my older work, and I'm excited as hell to share it with you! Here's a little taste!

Enjoy!

MONSTERS DON'T CRY

LIKE THE GIRLS IN THE MAGAZINES

"Jerry… Jerry! Get the fuck in here!"

Rapid footsteps.

"Yes, my love?"

"Don't give me that horse shit. Bring me my fucking pills. And hurry up! It fucking hurts!"

Natasha had her ear pressed to the door, her massive body curled up into a ball on the carpet. She chewed on the excess skin of her knee as she listened to her mother scream about pills and the pain in her new face.

That's what she called it: her new face. She had told Natasha all about it before she'd gone in for the procedure, violently running the brush through Natasha's wiry hair.

"And then your mommy will look young again," she'd said. "Just like she did on NICU. Your mommy was so beautiful back then." She pressed the teeth of the brush hard against Natasha's scalp as she raked it through her hair, but Natasha didn't flinch. "Some said I was the next big thing, you know. And then your daddy put *you* inside of me, and everything changed. Everything was ruined."

Natasha didn't understand what she meant by a new face. She wondered if her mother had her old face cut off and replaced with a younger, prettier one. Like the girls in the magazines. Every one of them so perfect, so beautiful. Natasha didn't blame her mother for wanting to look like them. Natasha understood.

If she could, she would rip all of their faces off so she could choose which one she wanted to wear each day. Like picking a hat or a pair of shoes—not that she had any of those either.

She would stare at the magazines for hours at a time, studying every inch of those girls, wishing she could be one of them, wishing she could wear clothes and makeup like them. If she looked like them, if she was pretty, everything would be better. Everything would be magical.

"What the fuck do you mean it's empty?" Her mother's voice brought Natasha back to the present, and she pressed her ear harder against the door. "Have you been stealing my shit, you fucking little bitch? Have you?"

"You finished them yesterday," Natasha heard her father say. "I told you that."

"Well call the doctor and refill it! I'm dying here." Her mother started to cry then, just like she always did when she wanted something. "Don't you care that I'm suffering? Aren't you supposed to be my husband?"

"Celeste, you—"

"Then fucking *help* me!"

"You've been taking too many pills. We can't fill the prescription for another week. I told you to follow the recommended dosage, but you—"

"Fuck you. Fuck you! You like watching me suffer, don't you? You always have. That's why you keep that… fucking mutant around, isn't it? Because you know it hurts me to look at her."

"She's our daughter. And she can hear you."

"She's a goddamn monster. We should have aborted her."

Slow, heavy footsteps.

"Where are you going? Get back here, you fucking pussy! Don't you fucking walk away from me!"

The footsteps stopped just outside of Natasha's door, and she scooted away, grabbed Honey from under her bed, and then squeezed the doll into her chest. But not too hard. Didn't want to break the porcelain.

Honey's face was even more beautiful than all the girls in the magazines, all the girls on TV. There was something about her smile, the way it was stuck that way and could never change, that Natasha found beautiful. As perfect as perfect could be. Permanent beauty. Not like her mom whose beauty had been shriveling away like a piece of old fruit.

The door eased open and Dad poked his

head in—he smiled at her the way he always did when her mother was having one of her episodes. Which was most of the time.

Natasha wished her mother would be more like the character she played on NICU. Grace—that was her name. So pretty, so nice. Always smiling and helping people.

An old episode of the now canceled show was playing on the small television in the corner of the room. The complete series on DVD sat atop the set, the only program her mother allowed her to watch.

"Hey, sweet pea," Dad said as he stepped into the room and shut the door behind him. "Your mother… She's in a lot of pain, baby. That's all. She's not herself."

Natasha mashed her lips together and shook her head, running her fingers through Honey's hair.

"You're right. She's being exactly like herself." He sat down on the bed and sighed, letting his head hang. He looked exhausted, gripping his knees and staring blankly at the floor. When he finally looked back up at her, he forced a smile and held out his arms. "Can I get a hug? Your hugs are the best hugs in the whole world. Did you know that, sweet pea? Your hugs could cure cancer."

Natasha couldn't help but giggle. She stood and turned her hips from side to side, one finger clamped between her teeth.

"Don't make me beg, now."

Natasha started toward Dad, slowly at first, then exploded into a sprint and tackled him, wrapping her thick arms around his neck and squeezing.

Instead of hugging her back, he patted her, slapping his hands over her shoulder blades and spine. Natasha peppered his bald head with kisses, basting it in lip-shaped saliva stamps.

"S-sweet pea… I can't… Natasha let me go!"

Natasha gasped and released him, then quickly scooted away from him. She fell hard off the bed, slamming the back of her head against the floor, but she kept shoving herself backward. Soft whimpers puttered from her throat as she watched her father writhe on the bed, his face pinched into a mask of pain.

"It's okay, baby," he said, wincing as he forced himself back into a sitting position. "I'm all right. Your dad's just not the young man he used to be, that's all."

Natasha nodded, but still kept her distance. She didn't like to see Dad hurt like that. Not him. Anyone but him. He didn't deserve to ever know what pain felt like.

"It's fine, Natasha. Please. Get your pretty butt back over here and hug your dad, okay? Just a little more gentle, that's all." Even when he smiled then, she could see the hurt in his face. His hands shook when he raised them.

Natasha sniffled, fingering the snot away from her tiny nose and wiping it over the back of her nightgown. She shuffled, dragging her feet, and eased herself onto the bed.

"I love you, sweet pea," Dad said as he wrapped his arm around her and kissed the side of her head. "I love you so much. Never forget that."

Natasha laid her head down on his shoulder and nodded. She traced Honey's smiling mouth with her finger.

Neither of them acknowledged her mother's continued screaming from the other room.

GIRLS ARE SUPPOSED TO BE PRETTY

"It's time for your bath."

On the floor, Natasha lay on her stomach, feet in the air and kicking as she flipped through the pages of the latest magazine. Dad had been teaching her to read when her mother was asleep, but some of the bigger words were still too hard.

This specific issue was comparing the dresses that all the gorgeous celebrity women had worn to the Oscars. Natasha didn't know what the Oscars was, but she wished she could be there. Wished she could wear a dress like the women in the pages, posing for pictures while everyone told her how beautiful she was.

Each and every dress was so breathtakingly stunning that Natasha found herself wanting to hurt the women who wore them. It wasn't fair that they got to drape their perfect, slim bodies into such glamorous fabrics. And every one of them probably had countless other dresses and lavish clothing that they took for granted. Purses and shoes and jewelry to accentuate their already flawless faces.

"Take those disgusting clothes off and get your ass to the bathroom. Hurry up." Her mother stood in the doorway, a smoldering cigarette hanging from her mouth. White bandages covered her entire face, except for her eyes, the tip of her nose, and her puffy, pink lips. She wore only a bra and panties. The leather whip hung from her other hand like a dead eel, its tip twirling just above the carpet.

Dad usually handled bath time. He would sit on the toilet with his back turned and read to Natasha as she washed herself.

Her mother hadn't bathed her in a long

time, and Natasha was glad for that. Always too rough, scrubbing Natasha's skin with steel wool, rubbing hardest over her breasts and between her legs, never satisfied until layers of skin were peeled away and the tub ran red with blood.

She used to say she was trying to wash the ugly off, that if she scrubbed hard enough, maybe Natasha wouldn't be so hideous. So embarrassing.

The whip was new. Natasha knew what a whip was from the Leather Slave magazine her mother had given her. Natasha didn't understand why her mother had given it to her, and figured it was probably a mistake, the strange and graphic magazine wedged in the center of the stack of Cosmopolitan and Style.

She was curious at first, flipping through the pages slowly, studying the images. Instead of fabulous dresses, the women wore leather straps and shiny boots. The men were tied up or hanging, mouths gagged, some with leather masks pulled tight over their heads.

It showed the women punishing the men, slapping and punching and pinching them, hitting them with whips and sticks, cutting them so the women could rub the blood over themselves, painting their naked breasts red. The men had these big fingers between their legs, not like the women, not like the hairy wet spot that Natasha had. And the women would touch the fingers, lick them, even bite on them until they bled.

Some of the pictures showed the men putting their big fingers inside of the women's wet spots. Or even their smelly spot.

Though it looked like it would hurt the women, they seemed happy. And the more Natasha stared at those pictures, the more she started to like them. When she looked at them, it made her chest and stomach tingle. Made her want to touch her chest, pinch her nipples. But more than anything, it made her wet spot wetter. Sometimes so wet it would drip.

One day, Natasha had reached down and let one of her fingers slide into her wet spot just like the men did in the magazine. It felt good at first, better than anything she could ever imagine. But then the good feeling turned bad, made her stomach swirl like she was going to puke. There was a stinging at the back of her throat, and she pulled her hand away from herself, forcing the vomit back down.

She'd hidden the magazine at the bottom of her stack, didn't ever want to see Leather Slave again, didn't ever want to think about naked men and their big fingers and her dripping, hairy wet spot. It was bad. It filled her with shame and humiliation, and she couldn't understand why anyone would want to feel that, why anyone would do those things to each other.

Just thinking about Leather Slave and seeing that whip hanging from Mom's hand made Natasha's stomach lurch and the back of her throat sting. A splash of hot liquid squirted against the back of her teeth, soaking her tongue, but she didn't dare let any of it out. Not with Mom watching. So she squeezed her eyes shut, gasped through her nose, and swallowed it all back down.

Natasha closed the magazine about the Oscars and set it neatly on top of her pile beside the television. Fashion and beauty magazines, the NICU DVD set—these were the only forms of entertainment her mother would allow.

MONSTERS DON'T CRY

"This is how girls are supposed to look," her mother would say, mashing Natasha's face into the glossy pages, shoving her down by the back of her neck. "Pretty. Girls are supposed to be pretty. Something you'll never be. You make me sick, do you hear me? Every fucking time I have to look at you, I want to puke."

Honey was a gift from Dad. The only new thing she'd ever owned. He had given it to her a long time ago. Said it was her birthday. Natasha didn't know what a birthday was, but she was happy to get the doll. And a chocolate cupcake.

She remembered Dad had laughed when she tried to eat the candle, fire and all. He took it away from her before she burned herself, then kissed her on the head and handed her the present. The box was almost as big as her at the time, all wrapped up in pretty pink wrapping with a silver bow on top.

"For you, sweet pea. A friend for my beautiful little girl. Or maybe a sister? Happy birthday."

The moment Natasha opened that box and saw Honey staring up at her, she felt less alone. She felt loved.

Natasha didn't understand why Dad let her mother treat them this way. Didn't understand how he could be so weak. She figured he was scared of her, even though he said he loved her.

Ever since Natasha could remember, her mother treated him like a slave. And he just took it, always did what she said. Natasha sometimes wanted to hit her mother. Rip her stomach open and stuff the insides down her throat.

But she couldn't do that. Dad loved Mom. And to hurt Mom would hurt Dad.

Natasha knew he loved *her* too—he told her all the time and was always so nice to her, even though he let Mom keep her locked up in her room.

But Natasha also knew Dad loved that woman more than anything. Not just because of what he put up with and how he let her treat him, but because of the way he looked at her. Natasha knew what that look meant, had seen it plenty of times on NICU, and it always led to romance.

Natasha wished Dad loved *her* as much as he loved her mother, but she was just happy to be loved at all. Dad was her best friend—

other than Honey—and she loved him so much it hurt the inside of her chest.

He didn't deserve to feel pain. Not ever.

Natasha faced her mother and curled her massive hands into boulders at her sides. Mom took a small step back, her eyes widening for a brief moment. But then she squinted, bared her teeth, and stormed across the room.

The cigarette sizzled as the cherry was pressed into the side of Natasha's neck.

But Natasha didn't wince. Didn't flinch. She just stared right into her mother's eyes as the heat was twisted into her flesh.

Slap!

"Don't you fucking look at me like that, you fucking freak! Now get your retarded ass in that tub." She flicked her wrist to make the whip crack, then reached up and grabbed the collar of Natasha's nightgown before tearing it off of her. The fabric got caught at Natasha's waist and hung down like a tattered tutu.

The television played the music from the opening credits of NICU. As much as she despised her mother, Natasha couldn't help but be fascinated by the show. She liked to imagine they were all acting just for her, trapped in her little box in her bedroom. Being forced to pretend for Natasha's own amusement—especially Mom. It made Natasha feel powerful, like she owned that part of her mother.

"Look at that," Mom said, shoving past Natasha so she could stand directly in front of the television. Her younger face faded in on the screen, and she held a tiny, pink baby in a light blue blanket, staring down at it with such love and worry. Her name slid into frame from the left and stayed there for about a second before the next actor had their turn.

Seeing that image always filled Natasha with anger. She knew her own mother didn't look at her that way, not even as a baby. She thought she remembered being born, squeezing her way out of her mother's moist, hot body. And she thought she remembered seeing her for the first time, seeing the disgusted look on her face.

But Natasha couldn't be sure those memories were real. She didn't need memories to know what her mother thought about her.

MONSTERS DON'T CRY

The woman never looked at Natasha with anything but hate and revulsion. The television version, Grace, was the only one who ever smiled or laughed or showed affection. It was almost as if her mother had used up all her joy and kindness playing Grace on the show, leaving nothing but ugliness and cruelty for her real life self.

"I was perfect back then. I was hot. Every man on that set wanted to fuck me. They wanted to fuck me so bad I could feel the heat swirling out of their pants. Every woman hated me because of it. I was a star. A rising fucking star. This show was only supposed to be the beginning. I was going to light up the fucking world."

Mom spun around so fast it was like her face emerged from the back of her head. The whip sliced through the air and cracked against Natasha's back, the tip wrapping around her ribs and stinging her on the breast.

Before Natasha knew what she was doing, she had her mother's throat in her hand. Squeezing. Turning the bandages red.

Mom's eyes widened until her lids disappeared into her sockets as she was lifted off the ground, legs kicking, red manicured nails raking across Natasha's arm.

Natasha could hear Dad's voice in her head then. As soft as a cloud of feathers floating in a silken breeze.

Don't hurt her, sweet pea. She's your mother. And I love her.

Natasha growled as she opened her fingers and let the choking woman fall into a heap at her feet. Mom gasped for breath, both of her hands at her neck now.

The television was just above Mom's head, another episode beginning. Grace was talking with a doctor. Flirting, smiling so wide that all her perfect white teeth showed.

Natasha reached down and picked up the whip. Her mother shook her head, sliding her ass across the carpet to get away. It looked like she was trying to talk, but she could only choke and cough.

Natasha gently set the whip down in Mom's lap before pulling her nightgown the rest of the way off and turning her back to her.

"That's right, you s-stupid fucking cunt." *Crack!*

"Now—now get your ass to the…" A

short pause. "What's this?"

Natasha slowly turned to face her mother, her heart sinking when she saw Honey being dragged out from under her bed. She gasped and immediately dropped to her knees, her eyes filling with tears as she watched her doll—her best friend and sister—dangling from Mom's talons.

"How did you get this? Your faggot fucking father? He give this to you?!"

All Natasha could do was whine, reaching her hands out. She never wanted anything more than to have Honey back in her grasp.

"What's the matter? Does the lil' monster want her dolly back?" Mom smiled through her bandages, though she was obviously still in pain.

Natasha whimpered, walked on her knees across the room, and lowered her forehead against the tops of her mother's feet.

Something hit her on the back of the skull. Natasha barely felt it, but it was the crashing sound that filled her with agony—the sound of breaking porcelain.

White and pink fragments rained down around her, followed by the cotton-filled body.

"Your daddy's next." *Crack!* "Now stand up. Hurry the fuck up! Get in that tub and scrub the shit off your skin!"

Tears stormed from Natasha's face, soaking into the tufts of cotton sticking out from Honey's mangled body. She grabbed it and squeezed, feeling her heart shatter inside her chest.

Crack!

The whip licked her with its fury, but that didn't matter. Her mother's screaming and cursing didn't matter either.

Natasha sifted through the shattered porcelain, the pieces becoming bloody as the jagged edges opened her fingertips. When the wide, white face smiled up at her from the debris, she nearly shouted.

Honey's brown marble eyes were gone, buried somewhere in the broken pieces, but it was still her face—whole and unbroken. Natasha didn't dare pick it up, or even acknowledge it, as she rose to her feet and wiped the snot from her nose.

The whip tore at her back as she trudged out the door and toward the bathroom.

TO BE CONTINUED

McHorror Stabby Meals

A Series of Fun-Sized Pocket Books

Other Stabby Meals:

STAB THE RABBIT: Have you ever wished you could meet your favorite cartoon character? Just yank them right from the TV into your living room? Go on adventures and cause some mischief together? For Boyd, this wish came true. And at first, it was all fun and games when his favorite cartoon bunny Harry Hare stepped out of the screen and into his home. That is, until Boyd's older, sadistic brother Randall got his hands on the animated rabbit. And started living out his most violent and twisted fantasies as he tortured Harry, inflicting a level of pain that is nonexistent in the universe of cartoons. The kind of suffering that is unique to our earthbound reality.

Will Boyd just stand by while his Saturday morning idol drowns in the colors of his agony? Or will he finally stand up to his maniacal bully of a big brother and try to rescue Harry Hare?

ABOUT THE AUTHOR

Shane McKenzie is a damn good husband and father, but a terrible homeowner. His front and back yards are covered in crispy, yellow grass and he's pretty sure his foundation is cracking. The only other thing he's really good at (he ain't a bad cook either) is creating disturbing, horrific stories to satisfy the depraved minds of people as fucked up in the head as him. If you're reading this… then you're one of those people, and Shane wants you to know how much he loves and appreciates you!